BEYOND IMAGINATION

2 __Beyond imagination__

BEYOND IMAGINATION

A thought-provoking novel inspired from mid-20th century events

Georgeta Simion - Potanga

Translation: Sophia Dediu

DERC Publishing House
Tewksbury (Boston), Massachusetts, U. S. A.

4 **Beyond imagination**

Library of Congress Cataloging in Publication Data

Potanga, Georgeta Simion

Beyond imagination
A thought-provoking novel inspired from mid-20th century events

ISBN-978-1-939757142

Editor's Note

After many years of literature teaching and writing, Prof. Georgeta Potanga presents this fascinating novel about astonishing and little known events from the mid-20th century in Eastern Europe, where Roosevelt, Churchill, Stalin, Hitler and many others had great influence and interests.

Based on real events, the author brings to life, with great talent, the vivacious atmosphere of those very difficult times. It is a novel made of shadows and light. The personages, under the Demiurge, succeed to step over the black stones of the physical universe, full feeling their destiny, with a profound humanity. The story follows the immediate antebellum events and the consequences of a brutal war in the life of three generations, showing that there are people who can express an extreme generosity, passing over any ethnic or religious barriers, in their desire to do good. The kindness, benevolence and sympathy of the personages extend universally and impartially to all human beings involved in this fascinating story.

Sophia Dediu worked immensely hard for this excellent translation, and we all thank her very much.

This is a novel which is read with pleasure and curiosity, and will delight all the readers who like historic events presented in an attractive literary style, and who want to discover many unfamiliar facts from the world's frenzied past.

Michael M. Dediu
U. S. A.

6 Beyond imagination

May, 1941. Teodora crossed the yard of her home, with small and sluggish steps, toward the carriage pulled at the front gate. She was trembling and her legs were uncertain, like stilts of wood, trying very hard to keep her body's balance.

Dressed in her best suit a little moldy, she wore on her head, plunked in a hurry, a light blue silk scarf, tied tightly under her chin in two nodes. On the back, out of one of the corner of her scarf dangled out a rich strand of her hair, braided in the model of a part of wheat, and it seemed that a rebellious part of her vertebral column came out in full view. Waves of tears flooded her cheeks glowing of an internal fever, braking out in sobs, gushing out from the depths of her tormented and confused being. She was holding tight to her chest the dead child, icy cold, swaddled in white festive diapers, with his head protected with a blue bonnet, wearing on the right-hand side, attached with a safety pin, perched on top, a large red bow.

Baby's cheeks, more pale than the holy beeswax, became completely cold, in a few hours, maintaining the pristine and chubby form of not long ago. The mother, with mechanical gestures, covered his little face with a fine kerchief woven from the most pure borage, for protection against the sun and wind.

Her husband, Ranger Dragomir, had just returned from the fair, and helped her to climb in the carriage. And he, too, was shocked and scared to death, living still under the impression of the discussion with the merchant Isidor, with whom agreed to a secret plan.

Seated near one another, swaying by the carriage' springs he pulled the horse trotted up slightly as the two spouses continued, each, their thoughts about the disaster that happened in the past few hours.

*

Dragomir remembered how he left, very early that morning to buy the necessary things for Mihăiță's funeral. He had thrown in the carriage two bags of wheat to be milled. Overwhelmed with the pain he had stopped first at the mill, where had been called by the mechanical voices of the mechanical tapping of the hammers, a sign that the miller had awoken early or he didn't sleep. A few farmers were already in the waiting line, discussing political issues; were worried about the atrocities perpetrated by the actual legionnaires, and also about the war which was drumming at the country's gate. The Ranger dumped the bags into a corner and without a word, in a silent grief, went out at once, and stopped in front of the Isidor's shop. Dragomir jumped out of the carriage blundering away, he pulled hard the bell's rope and waited. The merchant lingered a few moments, which for the Ranger seemed an eternity, then opened the door with obvious fear.

"You were? It's so good!" he said with a sudden vivacity for a moment, as a heavy burden was released from his heart.

The joy disappeared as soon as he closed the door and with a dull face sat down wearily on a chair. His furrowed face and the unkempt beard, like a clump of thistles, showed the figure of a man crushed by a heavy suffering. Nor the Ranger looked better. With a gloomy face, with a weak voice, and with the hands hanging seemed astounded by the pain and grief. Following Isidor, without waiting for an invitation, he sat without energy on the small chair beside the door.

The two knew each other from early childhood, because their parents lived in good relations and friendship. The Ranger Gherasim, Dragomir's father supplied the Isidor's family with fresh products and with fire wood. In its turn, Isidor senior offered to the Ranger's family the best goods. Although Isidor, the son was older than Dragomir by a year and a half, the difference between them wasn't visible. Isidor did two years at a commercial school in Iassy, turning back to take over the store. Dragomir was not outdone, he finished the forestry school. Both with some schooling, as much as they could, continued their friendship, meeting not only for business but also in private.

Dragomir married first and Teodora, his beautiful wife received as gift from the Isidor family a string of white beads, pearls imitation, imported from the east. At a wedding, the string of white bead caught everyone's attention.

A year later Isidor junior got married, bringing his wife from the Câmpulung region.

Berta, fine woman, with high school diploma, never mentioned about her studies, accepting without reservation, the friendship between the two families.

The name of the first child of the Isidor's family was Mihail. Few weeks later, Teodora gave birth to a boy christened Mihai. At three months the two children were introduced to each other, in an original way, placed near one another, in Mihail's crib. The boys were different in appearance. Mihail looked like Berta, skinny and blond, while Mihai grew up in the forest, bathed in fresh air and pampered by the sun, he was plump and lively. But both had something in common: blue eyes.

But the sky, jealous, sipped forever Mihai's blue eyes, taking him away in its empire.

Dragomir's confession about his child's death united the two of them by an excruciating pain and at the same time, like at a silenced signal, they raised their arms to the sky in rapture, asking for a bit of mercy.

Locked in the shop, they had a lengthy talk for more than an hour disregarding the bustle of the street and the ringing of the bell.

Suddenly, the Jew stopped breathing astounded by a thought. His mind was sparkling and his light-gray face was beaming as lighted by an interior radius; a brilliant and savior idea just hit him. Dragomir was listening.

Isidor was talking slowly, weighing each word, with some sort of fear, as the walls may have ears. Berta was called up to this discussion. She a delicate lady, now pale, with dark circles and the eyes red from crying and sleepless had Mihail in her arms.

Dragomir looked attentive at the blond boy with big eyes, broken like from the sky's sapphire, tired and agitated as his parents. According to their plan he was to replace Mihai, the dead child of the Ranger.

*

The legionnaires' rebellion in January, aimed mainly to hunt and decimate the Jews in Romania. Because in the town of Pungeşti there was already a nest of the legionary movement, the Jews from the city felt and they knew very well that their days were counted.

The plotted plan in the merchant's shop went beyond any one's imagination; it assumed courage and major risks and which the two of them took with great responsibility. Their secret, sealed through a sacred oath, followed the way of some unwritten laws, but with compelling human value. Dragomir came in the town with a purpose which crumbled like a sandcastle. He no longer needed the coffin nor other objects necessary for a funeral.

The Ranger came out of the shop running, and jumping as a spring directly in the carriage. The horse sensed the master's hurry and rising his two front feet was waiting for his command.

"Let's go home!" said the ranger.

The animal, smart, turned the carriage around and started to gallop. The man was trying to gather his thoughts and, in particular, to find the best way to tell to his wife the plan established with Isidor. The ideas were fighting over in his head but there was no time for imaginary fighting, because the horse stopped in front of the gates, which were not fully opened, a sign that he was going to go away quickly.

As he entered through the door Teodora looked surprised seeing his face changed and without any shopping done.

With the soul ransacked by the child's death and the news that flew through the town like black birds of prey, Dragomir told his wife about the plan plotted with Isidor, plan that should be implemented as soon as possible.

All was carried out at the lightning speed so that the woman traumatized of pain had little time to say yes or not. She dressed in a hurry, then took the dead child from the table, extinguished the candles, and followed blindly her husband. While in the house, Teodora taken by surprise did not react in any way, now seated in carriage, together with her husband, she came to her senses and her wise mind began to decipher the ideas and the events as they were to take place. In her mind, on a side she would obey to this idea of her husband, but on another side she would not. "How to swap the children?" and "what kind of exchange is that, giving a dead baby and getting one alive!" This deed went so far beyond her imagination. "How she couldn't have her boy buried following a Christian ritual after which he'd become an angel in six months!", "What will Mihăiţă do all alone buried in the Jewish cemetery at the edge of the town?" But when her thoughts turned on the other side, the ideas changed. "Mihai is an angel, without going back in time and space. God wanted him, and maybe today He demands that we save a life just as innocent as his. Let it be as God wishes." Her tears were flowing streaming down, Teodora sighed, squeezing tight the baby to her chest with so much power as though she wanted to revive him by transferring to him a portion of her soul and her life.

Her thoughts gushed over her again bringing in the foreground the tragic events that occurred in the last hours.

*

All day Mihai cried continuously and uncontrollably. He refused the breast milk, he couldn't sleep and the gentle rocking on his mother soft arms no longer calmed him down as it did in the past. The same happened with their first child, Dumitru.

"Maybe the forestry cottage in which they live is a damned place?" She never gave a thought about this before. Every year during the big holidays, the priest came and read his prayers and sprinkled saint water all over the house. "Why this should happen to them?" Dragomir waited as laying on sharp thorns, that the night passes more quickly and at dawn he was going to run to pharmacy. Seldom happen that the medicines prescribed by Mr. Pharmacist Lucian to fail.

Once the night fall and after all this crying and turmoil, the child went into a smooth sleep and unnatural. The parents, more calm, were on the watch while drifting in moments of sleep as birds on twigs, leaving their hearing in charge. In the quiet room was a silence as in a tomb. Teodora, with steps of a cat, went closely to the boy and looked at him carefully. The child, with a pale face, was sleeping unmoved and only the thumb of his left leg was moving in a nervous tic. She kissed his cold forehead and staring at the child panicked.

"Good heavens", she screamed, "our child stopped breathing".

Dragomir jumped and touched with his palm the boy's icy forehead.

The woman with the hands shaking lighted in hurry a candle, anxiously looking at his thumb which was moving increasingly less, as a spring unlocked from the main power supply. But the thumb stiffened and with that the last hope faded. For them remained only candle's flame and their tears.

Dragomir's head felt flooded of painful bloody wires, which was like a rubber ball that changed its form continuously. His house was adorned with a dozen of lighted candles. But the real light didn't come from the wax of the candles but it was a great- strange glint lowered from the sky, in which was floating slow a group of angels among which was also Mihai. In their despair, the parents stretched out their arms toward him and called him. But the angels don't talk, they communicate only through light.

Overwhelmed by pain, exhausted, they looked at each other as two rocks, trying to control their bitterness that dispersed in huge waves into their lives.

They were aware that no human power can bring back Mihai to the earthy feelings and yet shuddered at every flicker of the candlelight. The candle was burning quietly under the wooden icon of the saints of Mihail and Gavril, and spreading vibrations of tranquility, which, unfortunately did not touched their souls.

Dragomir knew what has to be done because it passed only one year from the death of the first son and Isidor knew very well everything that's needed for any wedding, christenings or funeral.

He dressed quickly in his ranger uniform hugged his wife and went out just at the dawning of the day. There was silence. The wind gathered all the clouds in a place, as a good architect, and then had hitched itself in its invisible palace.

At the master's voice, the horse, shaking its mane, placed its muscles in motion accepting with pleasure the soft harnesses of skin. They moved a few steps, two rounds of the carriage's wheels, next to the barn's door from where Dragomir pulled and threw in the back of the carriage two bags of wheat.

"Let's go, Murgule!"

The horse started at once looking at the new whip which his master never used it on him

All alone at home, Teodora gathered her scattered energies because there were too many things to be done. First she washed the child, and then she dressed him with new cloth received at christenings from godparents. While waiting for the coffin's arrival she placed the boy on the larger room on the table. She lighted a new series of candles and placed in the middle the large candle from his christening ceremony. It was nicely decorated with flowers and with blue, red, and white ribbons. The flowers kept in a cool and dark place dried nicely before became wilted and now seemed glazed.

The window from the East lightened and a silver ray coming from the sky lighted the dead child's face. The darkness of the night started to scatter through the valleys and the stars dimmed above the shadows of the clouds on the serene vault. "Did Mihai's star fell?"

The forestry cottage in which they lived was far away from the town. Their parents and relatives were even further, in Gârceni. Only the next day they could send word about the calamity that hit again their young family.

When the Ranger returned from town, the whole planning for funeral and for which Teodora spent a lot of thinking melt like a snowflake, the things taking an unexpected turn. They were supposed to go to Pungeşti.

*

The horse trotted towards the city smoothly not to shake the masters.

The tears and sobs broke involuntarily bringing Teodora to the sad reality. She embraced tighter and harder the baby to her breast kissing his cold and lifeless forehead.

"We're approaching the city and please wipe off your tears. We must not leave any trace of suspicion in connection with our plan."

He raised the kerchief from the child's face trying to memorize the baby's face. This was the last time he would see him.

The sun rise courageous and swarms of small insects were flying in discreet murmur, bathing into its light. The leaves of the trees started to open up and everything smelled of green since from the Saint Gheorghe, when the forest ended.

Perhaps all plants and living creatures of the Earth have a soul as people, pain or joy, subject to the nature's laws, which dominates our existence.

The horse turned left to the biggest church from Pungeşti. The earthquake from 1940 demolished one of the towers. The roof showing small holes was unrepaired and gave the impression of a deep sadness.

At the entry into town, the road turns suddenly in a paved road with wide sidewalks, well-marked along which walked slowly a gendarme continuously moving his baton.

When they saw him, the spouses gasped with fear, the blood freeze in their veins, however they controlled their temper.

"Good day and best wishes for the better." said Dragomir respectfully to the gendarme.

"Good day and best wishes to you too, Mister Rabger, you came up to town with the wife and the child?"

"Yes, we want to do some shopping."

"Well, you do, because soon you'll not have from where to buy anymore."

The gendarme was right; he as an official person, who embraced the green shirts, knew more.

As soon as they walked away a few steps from the gendarme sighed relief. But before their fear went away, another ice cold shower drizzled on their spinal cord.

In the front of Isidor's shop stopped a white car. The driver, who past his first youth, tired and quite uninterested was napping with his head down over the steering wheel.

Dragomir jumped from the carriage and indirectly found out from the driver the reason for his stop in front of the shop.

"The merchant's baby, said the driver grumpy, is gravely ill and Mr. Doctor Manea has been called urgently by telegraph; but you can enter."

The Ranger pulled gently the rope of the bell from the entrance and waited.

Immediately, in the doorway, came Isidor, with a benevolent smile and with friendly gestures invited them in the shop. From the shop with the doors locked, they passed into the next room, a huge living room with sculpted furniture, paintings and Persian rugs. At a sign everybody sat down in massive leather armchairs. The Doctor Teodor Manea was watching with interest the new guests about which he had heard, trying to penetrate beyond their appearance, with his medical knowledge. The young couple made a good impression. He, sober, seemed a man attached to the family and also to his profession. She, dressed clean, even exceeding expectations, despite the heavy suffering kept her optimism and confidence.

Berta held in her arms the baby who was asleep and greeted them without any move, just from her eyes. On her face was visible the pain, and compassion for the death of Mihai.

There was an urgent matter, so Isidor, without further introduction, passed directly to the subject of the appointment.

"Brother Dragomir", he began, "our bargain did not undergo any change, the plan will remain forever; we are expecting difficult days ahead. Berta and I entrust you with all our love and hope our son who will be called Mihai. Mr. Doctor Manea, is a participant in our secret, and certifies today this oath. From this moment he becomes your friend also and his door will be forever open for you and for our child. Our seminitia shall bless the human deed which all of us commit now, and especially us, confronting with dignity the history's errors, assuming the most dangerous risks".

Teodora, as a lesson learned, made the first step toward the fulfillment of this agreement established in the morning by the two men. She stood up, kissed the dead child placing him on the table, trying to cope with the difficult inside wail. Her youth and self-discipline helped her to control the river of tears, which seemed to flood all her body. She approached Berta receiving in her arms the baby. There was a moment of maximum tension, and each of them expressed their emotions in different ways. The Doctor was looking with a hidden sorrow at the scene. Dragomir and Isidor embraced discretely wiping their tears, which couldn't be halted. Berta's body and soul were shaking and she remained speechless.

The two mothers, were holding in the middle the child alive, hugging each other in the same time and did not dare to separate. Their tears, rushing in streams, interlaced their salty dripping on Mihail's head. The silence was broken by a whimper of a hungry child who was searching with his rosy lips on the left and right.

"I'll get immediately the bottle," said Berta coming to her senses, "because lately with all this anger and sleepless nights, my milk disappeared."

"Mister Doctor," interposed shyly Teodora, "can I breastfeed him, if you give me permission?"

The Doctor smiled being influenced by her youth and the overflowing health displayed without ostentation by the woman, made only a gesture of approval.

Teodora, at her request, accompanied by Berta entered the bathroom where she rinsed her breasts with cold water and milked out the stale milk which had gathered for twenty-four hours. Her white slip and also the blouse were already wet from drops of milk escaped from her breasts round as melons.

The young mother sat down on an armchair on a side, and leaving the embarrassment aside, she took gently the child in her arms and gradually approached his breast to his face. Mihai, attracted by the smell of sweet milk, fast without special invitation, caught the breast nipple, sucking avidly, as afraid that he'll lose it. The milk, plentiful flowed almost alone in the baby's mouth and from time to time escaped through the corner of his small lips into small white locks cleaned fast and gently by his mother with a small handkerchief trying not to interrupt the feast.

After a while, the child was swallowing more and more rarely, a sign that the hunger was quelled.

Satisfied, without releasing the source of his milk, he paused, looking as in a mirror into the blue eyes of his new mother, who looked to him total reliable. A smile and an enjoyable prattling expressed the health and safety of the baby.

But there was no time to lose, the protocol had been concluded and the exchange sealed with tears, hopes and sobbing.

Mihai was dressed over his clothes with a white outfit a blue cap with red bow perched on top. Teodora held him tightly to her chest with love trying to swallow the tears that sprang continuously, without her permission.

The body of the true Mihai was left at the mercy of the destiny on the table in the living room. Soon he will be wrapped in a shroud and prepared for another ceremony.

In the shop, placed beside the door, were waiting a few large packets, supposedly the Ranger's shopping.

"Brother," said Isidor, "take and please keep this box in which it is the Star of David, the symbol of my nation. It has been kept for generations. I offer it to you with all my heart for our son, to bring you luck and health!"

Then he reached out to a shelf taking a brown leather bag, well stuffed.

"In this is a handful of money for Mihai expenses, and in these boxes, small gifts for you."

Few times Dragomir wanted to say something, but each time Isidor tapped him on the back, a sign meaning that he understood his thoughts and the unspoken words.

Everyone lived dramatically the painful moments. The women still crying looked at each other with an unspoken goodbye from their babies.

Isidor unlocked the door and helped the Ranger to arrange the boxes into the carriage.

The woman climbed in the carriage and sat in the same place, holding tightly to her chest the sleeping child. The horse started to move taking the road toward the house. The sun was warm and was anticipated a beautiful afternoon. Lazy rays were inundating the streets and the yards.

They passed by the same gendarme who was in conversational mood, and tried to find out some fresh information.

Those on the carriage were no longer trembling with fear, as when they met him earlier, and the child from the mother's arms was dead, but they didn't want to lengthen the discussion.

"So, how is the merchant Isidor doing?"

"They were saddened and troubled because of the gravely ill child." answered Dragomir very sober.

"Yes, we do know. They brought Dr. Manea, the best in Vaslui.

"Good day!" came the flattering answer from the Ranger without stopping the horse. Then he pressed it and continued faster on the road.

The Gendarme remained with a smile on his lips, showing a belly inflated like a turkey.

The horse was walking leger in no hurry. His masters were no longer rushing. Teodora was holding the child asleep in her arms, but her thoughts, wondered in disarray without rest, trying the reconciliation with the destiny. In six months, Mihai brought them as much happiness as the amount of water in a large ocean, and suddenly, everything dried out reducing only to a tear.

The all mighty in who's perfection we trust, has Himself his caprices, justified or unjustified, giving us, with unlimited generosity unsuspected things, which moves us closer to the supreme haven of hope. Sometimes, the whole demiurge destroyed everything, leaving behind particle of dust, and memories.

The woman, in her immeasurable grief, was counting the trees on the side of the road unable to communicate with them, not in words, nor with the thoughts, but only with her imagination. With her eyes full of tears looking through the trees' leaves, she had the illusion that Mihai laughs together with the sparrows and the goldfinches.

"Mihăiță!" she called, looking in vain.

Dragomir turned his head toward her understanding her motherly pain. Teodora, roused from her painful fantasy, getting back to reality.

After a while, near the cottage, Teodora raised slightly the handkerchief from the child's face. The sunlight suddenly caressed the pale cheeks and the baby opened his eyes, opened his little mouth like a chick of swallow stretching out his small body wrapped in nappies. The two looked at each other in the light of the sun getting the feeling of mother and son. The mother did not let him wait too long offering to him another portion of milk directly from the source. The child, rocked by the snail-slow of the carriage, was sucking quietly, not hastily, marveling at the abundance of food which was missing the past few weeks.

When Teodora said "That's enough now, mommy, you eat enough", her husband looked at them with fatherly love, momentarily forgetting that Mihai actually is Mihail.

They already entered in the forest, in the nature's harmonious surroundings in which the grass, flowers, trees, insects, and people live and enjoy in equal measure, protected by the whole universe.

The horse stopped right in front of the large oak gates, sculpted by the nearby masters. Dragomir jumped from the carriage, pulled the latch and the gates opened as two huge hardcover of a book. In just a few steps the carriage stopped again in front of the stairs.

Assisted by her husband the woman stepped down with great care not to shake the baby who was asleep again in the clean air and the strong smell of the forest at the begging of spring.

The horse turned his head, as usually, to smell the little buddy. He shook his mane, snorting his nostrils when he noticed so much change to the child that happened only in one day. But its mind did not rationalize.

Teodora entered the house; put the child in the big bed. Opened wide the windows to let out the smell of burned candles, which was felt in the room.

It was a new start for all of them.

Dragomir downloaded the boxes and stored them in the entrance hall. He then went to take care of his faithful animal which went twice in the city in that day.

The child was sleeping, smiling in his sleep, and dreaming harmless dreams. The parents opened the boxes.

First carefully they opened the box it which was "The Star of David". About the king David, Dragomir knew something and began to tell to Teodora:

"In olden times, thousands of years ago, the philistines started war against the Israelites. The philistines' trusted man was a warrior, a superman called Goliath. The giant, secure on his physical powers asked to fight first with a solder selected from the Israelites army. A young shepherd named David had become known for his skill with which he killed, without weapons, the lions and bears that came to steal the sheep. The legend says that David's fame reached the king's ears.

At the enemy's proposal, the king decided that the special fighter would be David. In such circumstances, of great importance and liability, the king has endowed David with his fighting armor, composed also of a helmet of brass, and a sword adorned with precious stones. The young fighter preferred to remain dressed in his shepherd cloth and armed only with his stick and sling. As cannonballs he collected from the river five stones and put them in his bag.

In the battle field, waiting for the opponent, Goliath was displaying his anxiousness waving his threatening sword. He couldn't believe when from the Israelite army showed up a young man blond who wanted to fight him with a sling. He burst in a roar of laughter and amusement. He ignored the proverb saying "who laughs at last, laughs best".

David wasn't intimidated by the giant's attitude. With a smile on his lips and much calm, using his sling threw at the giant a stone that hit him right on his forehead sending him to the ground face down. Without giving him respite, rushed and taking his sword cut his head off. The enemies ran away and for long time after they stayed away from the sons of Israel.

At thirty years of age, David became king, followed to the throne by his son Solomon, well known for his wisdom.

"How do you know all this?" asked Teodora with curiosity.

"Isidor told me one evening sitting at a beer; but I read them also in the Bible, which we had at home", said Dragomir.

The man was holding "The Star of David" in the hand marveling at the strange light that radiated from it. Never had he seen such jewelry. The woman, curious, took it herself in the palm of her hand, experiencing an odd feeling. They both were thinking the same thing: where to hide the precious object?

After much thoughtfulness they have found the right place. Dragomir cut with a chisel and a hammer on the eastern beam a small niche of the size of the box; a true secret hiding place. The place has been re-arranged such that no one would guess that there is a hiding place.

Then he emptied on the table the content of the leather bag offered by Isidor. They both gasped fearfully. With the money from the bag one could raise five children not just one. The amount of money in front of them, relative to the wages of a Ranger seemed immense. In fact, there were the savings of merchant's wise family gathered in a few years. The paper money, carefully folded, did not occupy a large volume, so they placed them next to their small savings and their valuable papers under the central beam.

The golden coins rolled in freedom on the table's perimeter under the astonished eyes of the two.

Teodora remembered that her grandparents also have well hidden, in secret, a few coins of gold saved for grandchildren or for rainy days. But these were different and nothing that she saw in her life.

Two coins, with the face of the tsar Nicolae of Russia, they looked new the time's taint didn't touch their faces. Another golden coin bigger had engraved the effigy of Napoleon I. More cheerful and novel were the French cocks which displayed the incrustation of a rooster, which seemed alive, and ready to sing. There were numerous Turkish coins "Mahmudels" used also on these parts of the world during the second half of the XIX century.

Both of them were looking at the gold in fear. "If someone finds out about their treasure?" "How, where, and how long will they have to hide the treasure to be safe?" Returning to reality they were thinking that they need to find a hiding place about which not even a fly should know.

Dragomir went into the barn; he poked around on the dusty shelves and old objects until he found exactly the box that he was in search for. He didn't know what for was that box used before. It was a manmade box of foil of zinc, a little rusted here and there. The hinges and the latch were rudimentary but in good condition. The box became the ideal place for their treasure. Teodora wiped off the dust, and then carefully, placed in the coins, one at a time covering them with a clean handkerchief.

They climbed in the attic looking everywhere through all corners. The floor of the attic was brand new of plank of beech wood. Under the eaves, above the verandah the planks of the floor were smaller. He took away a small board, placed the box in and put the board back. Not even a sharp eye would have noticed that there was something hidden.

*

About treasures, in general, there were many mysterious legends, some belonging to the black magic; the spouses didn't like them, and they were uneasy about these.

The elders were talking that on the night of resurrection the hidden treasure burn in flame without destroying the place. Those who ran, attracted by the flames, and reached the flaming point, didn't find anything, instead they got lost wandering around for hours until they made it through.

A lad from their native township saw an elder man who was burying coins in the graveyard. He was speaking some sort of a message or a curse that the young man didn't understand. When the old man left the lad went to the place in question and furrowing in the earth, he found three gold coins and took them home. The legend says that after that night after night, a ghost showed at the window, and a human demanded his golden coins back. To regain his peace, the lad went to the grave yard and buried the coins in the same lace. The ghost did not show up again to disturb his nights.

Teodora recalled that as a child, when she was in the fourth grade, in her history book, two pages enshrined the treasury "The hen and the chicks" from the township of Pietroasele, from the Buzau county. The treasure was discovered incidentally by two masons. As all the reassures the "The hen and the chicks" has a troubled history. The total number of pieces that made up this discovery was twenty two and their weight was measured in kilograms having various forms a large platter and a small platter, kettles, baskets, necklaces, birds, al made of solid gold embellished with precious stones, blue, red, yellow and white.

The two discoverers tried to sell for profit parts of the treasure. They destroyed without pity a good part of the beautiful objects and sold them.

But the magical and fantastically power that surrounded the treasure spread amongst those who destroyed it only curses and troubles. Houses burned, children died, incurable diseases were hurled in the families who thought that they will become reach by stealing the saint gold. Scared by the misfortunes that diverted over them they returned the remaining parts of the treasure back at the place where it was discovered. The state authorities recovered what was left, only twelve pieces. Researchers found later when the treasure was partially recovered, that it belonged to a Gothic tribe. The inscriptions indicate the ownership: "The holy property of the Goths". The pieces have been worked at Constantinople in various workshops by skilled masters and have been used as worship objects.

During the First World War, the Romanian government has decided to carry the treasure in a safe place, to Moscow. Subsequent events which have devastated Russia, and instated a different form of government haven't allowed the immediate return of the treasure to Bucharest. After long negotiations that lasted for decades "The hen and the chicks" has been recovered in 1956, and placed at the Museum of History.

Connecting with the history lesson from the book the teacher Costică Chirițescu told his students another legend known in the whole world. It is about the great treasure hidden in the lake Baikal.

*

Coming down from the attic, Teodora was thinking that their situation does not fit the legends about which they heard or read. The golden coins received from Isidor and hidden in the box were earned money saved by generations that worked very hard for them. They were offered to them with love, best wishes and good luck. It was, in fact Mihai's treasure.

The child was sleeping quietly, dreaming sweet dreams. Sometimes he smiled or moving his raspberry lips miming that he is sucking. The parents were looking down at him with great love striving to forget forever that Mihai actually is Mihail, the son of Isidor and Berta.

They returned to the boxes and continued to unpack them. In the first box there were cloths for all ages of a child. Teodora placed them neatly side by side, on the bed. There were slippers, boots, shoes, heats of different colors all arranged like in a store. "Lord", was Teodora thinking, "our child will be dressed like a king!" Then her mind became confused when she remembered that, in fact, the baby that she gave birth to was wrapped in a shroud waiting to be lowered in the ground's dust from which God created us. But the oath remained sacred: this and only this is her child.

The following box contained nappies white as the snow, towels, blankets, all made of simple cotton or mercerized.

In the third package, there were several fabrics, stockings, female slips and other things that made the eyes of the young woman shimmer with pleasure. Her eyes remained glued to a brand-new knee-long fur jacket with a foreign label.

Will she have the courage to wear it ever? A similar one she had seen on the pharmacist's wife, beautiful woman, with higher education and with a certain rank in society. But she, the modest wife of a ranger, asked: what for to dress with such expensive coat? But, who knows what the future holds for her!

Dragomir wasn't forgotten either. The most bulky boxes contained things for him: two suites, footwear, heavy overcoat, rain overcoat, several shirts and a few gadgets. There was even a brand-new Ranger suite.

The Ranger was thinking "I wonder how we will be able to thank to our benefactor and friend?" Momentarily, all good things were only on their side. They had been given a child in a tragic moment, helping them to pass more easily over suffering and pain. And as if it hadn't been sufficient, Isidor gave them money and other necessary things. Their black glumness turned little by little in incoherent light. Bizarrely, they received back the child, trying very hard to inoculate the thoughts that Broken stems back in sleepy child, trying hard to inoculate the thought that Mihail is Mihai.

The turmoil of the two of them ended when the baby's sleepy voice, as a ring of a bell, wake them up to reality. Everything was left aside and Teodora, with a wide smile, picked up the baby in the light and kissed him with love on both cheeks. She unwrapped gently the baby to change his diapers. Mihai, left naked, sensed the freedom and moved his arms and legs as though he wanted to swim. His parents were watching his movements identical with Mihai's. Wrapped in clean diapers, the baby enjoyed with pleasure mother's milk. Then fatigued, let go from his mouth the breast which he was holding with both hands. It was his property. With delicacy, the mother, covering her breast, raised the boy in the vertical position patting softly on his back. He looked at Dragomir demanding to be taken in his arms. That was all Dragomir waited for. He took the baby in his arms and went out into the yard to talk.

"This is a turkey, and the other one which sings is a rooster." The child twittered something, perhaps wanted to say that he understood. He walked into the stable and introduced him to the horse. Mihai stretched his small arm trying to caress the velvet skin of the horse, which closed his eyes for pleasure. They walk through the entire yard telling him all the animals' names, as he did with the other Mihai.

A wind with smell of the forest tickled baby's nostrils making him sneeze. Dragomir took him inside and left him in mother's care, who didn't yet finished placing the things in the closet which seemed now too small.

Teodora put the baby in the bed, and in a low voice, she murmured a lullaby which put the baby in a sleep mood. In a few minutes Mihai fall asleep, playing in his dream with the rooster, turkey, pigeons and other poultry to which has been introduced.

Dragomir went to make a tour through the woods. Early the next morning he had to go to town. He knew that he could not attend Mihai's burial ceremony, but he wanted to find out the place intended for the grave of the eternal child's sleep.

Returned from the forest he found everything in the most perfect order. Mihai, bathed and fed was about to fell asleep. He would sleep and he wouldn't sleep, was playing with the hands in the air as he would draw something. His parents were watching carefully, conversing in low voices problems that had to be resolved on the following day.

The candle was still burning and will go out only after forty days, the tradition must be preserved.

They lived a rough day, checkered and sprinkled with hot tears. Finally, when managed to put their heads on the pillow, they fell asleep, as logs. The baby was sleeping a profound sleep along with his parents.

In the morning he wake up first and his voice sounded as a call of awakening, preparing his lips for sucking. After breakfast the mother, with gentleness and affection was patting his back and kissed his cheeks and forehead. Followed the walking around, holding him tightly, speaking to him, and showing the things around the room. When she took him outside in the forest's fresh and clean air in short time he went to sleep, and then she took him inside and put him in the big bed. Then she continued her chores. From time to time she burst in tears, crying again and, shedding her anger.

Next day Teodora did not want to go to their friends Isidor and Berta empty handed. She prepared a cut turkey, well cleaned and ready to be put to boil in the pot, some fresh cheese, eggs, dried plums, walnuts and apples stored in hay, all arranged in a beautiful basket, covered with-n clean towel. Dragomir placed the basket in the carriage and with the sun shining in his in face, departed for town.

The horse, rested now, was going at trot, listening careful the master's commands. Dragomir was surprised to see that when they entered the town at the corner street the same gendarme greeted him.

"Good day", said the Ranger.

"Same to you," said the law's man, "again in town? You know, here, serious things happened. Mr. Isidor's child is dead and today will be the funeral."

"God protect him, I didn't know. I was going to him, and now I'm thinking that in this situation I shouldn't needlessly intrude."
"Come on, Murgule!"

The horse guessed the real intension of his owner and stopped in front of the shop. Dragomir rang and Isidor dressed in black received him with the same sadness in his eyes. As soon as they entered the door was locked behind them.

"Teodora sent you some of our food," said with affection the Ranger.

Berta took the food and returned in few minutes with the basket filled with other products.

"Our child is well, eats and sleeps well. We pray that God will keep him this way", said in a whisper Dragomir. "We" come Sunday so you can see him."

On the table, in a beautiful coffin was resting in his eternal sleep their child, the real Mihai.

The ranger left and went to the mill to recoup the bags with flour. There he heard only bad news. A part of the Jews from the neighboring townships have been removed and sent to Vaslui and squeezed in a couple of slums.

From there Dragomir wandered through town leaving the carriage in Chiriac's yard. He invented several reasons, so he can go at the edge of the town to the Jewish cemetery.

Close to noon a small funeral cortege enters the cemetery. All were mourning and their faces were sad. The child's casket was lowered in the crypt of Isidor's family. A funeral monument of black marble with carved inscriptions was watching over the body covered to earth.

Now, Dragomir learned where Mihai's grave is, but he realized that wasn't prudent to make any reckless gesture. He left the cemetery and strode toward Chiriac's court where he had left the carriage. In the carriage he found a child's crib and a mirror of crystal well packaged. Chiriac himself didn't know who put these objects in Dragomir's carriage.

It was already afternoon and the Ranger started on the road toward canton.

Teodora with the child in her arms, waited for him in the courtyard. He told her that he found the grave, and promised that they'll go back together in a while to see the grave. Until then, next Sunday, they will go to visit Berta and Isidor who will be waiting for them.

Now, the township Pungeşti began to attract them more and more to be closer to where Mihai slept his forever sleep.

*

The approximately seventy-five Jewish families, who lived in Pungeşti, were well organized, with a school in Yiddish language, a synagogue, cemetery, bath and other traditional amenities necessary to a civilized life, corresponding to the respective historic moment.

The shops, side by side, crowded with goods for all pockets, were lined up on Main Street opposite the main institutions of the town. In particular, the manufacturing shops and groceries were all in big demand. Isidor, Zisu, Moise, Lupu and Haim were the most respected merchants. Their shops were very attractive because of the large variation and the quality of their merchandise. The two bakeries functioned non-stop and barely could satisfy the demand. The luxury tailor was the prerogative of the intellectuals and the wealthy. Ordinary people were going to the less expensive tailoring shops were the goods were more accessible.

At the periphery of the township were located the carpentry, the blacksmiths, boilermakers, and they all use the local resources. Tenths of youngsters from the neighboring townships became apprentices, trying to still the secrets of the master craftsmen, and preparing themselves to compete with them no too long in the future. The merchants, settled in Pungeşti, thoroughly supported economic and cultural power of the township and of the surrounding villages. For a good merchant there was never, in terms of time, the notion of late or too early. The merchants welcomed you at any time of the day or night with the same pleasant smile. The needy people enjoyed the price reductions and late payments. The Jews were esteemed and respected by all the villagers for the honor, diligence and their skills.

The legionary movement and the war have faltered the peaceful life, and the growth of the old Moldavian Township. A nest of legionaries, which became every day, more and more aggressive. The head of the group was the landowner Jack himself, who was of a not too tall stature, his face furrowed by deep wrinkles, caused by the permanent frightening soul, dressed in green shirt, mostly riding, whipping the whip to the right and to the left. Passersby, knowing his habit were staying out of the way. The judge, and the mayor, did not dare to oppose as long as he was wearing the green shirt.

Among the intellectuals who were neutral in politics, was also the pharmacist, Lucian Hălăuceanu gentle and kind man who unconditionally and professionally helped those in needs. The locals considered him a doctor. His tips and his remedies were always helpful having the desired effect.

The pharmacist, conscientious and dedicated professional, made himself available for any requests at any time, courteous and happy that another good deed was born. Tall, thin, with clear eyes, permanently displayed a benevolent smile, urging everyone to discuss their problems, without embarrassment. He learned several secrets because people confined in him. The revealed secrets had a status of confessions and the patients appreciated his sincere and honest character.

*

Lucian Hălăuceanu was from Roman. His parents, Jewish, owned a small restaurant, on the Garrison Street. From high school he started to help his father in the restaurant as waiter. He was quick at work; confident in everything he was doing. The other two employees could not keep up with him. When he became student in Iassy continued working during holidays in the restaurant.

During his last year in college, at a colleague birthday party he met a young lady, the daughter of an impoverished nobleman from Hălăuceni.

Olguța Hălăuceanu studied at the "Lady Helen" Pension in Iassy. She was a beautiful girl, well-mannered and any young man would accept her friendship.

Her father, lord Costache, was searching right and left looking for a groom, an older man, and rich to lift them up from their needs. The girl, however, was decided not to sell her beauty to a man who was in the threshold of youth fade to hold on the family blazon.

From the first moments Lucian was enchanted by her charmed image; never put the question if Olguța is Jewish or Christian. Although he had beautiful colleagues at the University, none attracted him particularly. Olguța's black eyes, round and shiny insistently were looking with wonder and insistence at the man in front of her as if she knew him for a long, long time. Her high forehead freed the delicate muscles of her face tanned by the sun. Her round mouth was in perfect harmony with the eyes. She laughed with her whole being making her black hair wave as the tails of young wild horses on a prairie.

Lucian hypnotized, was trying a feeling that inundated his heart and mind.
The whole evening they talked, they laughed, they danced as though they knew each other before they were born. Maybe, indeed, they existed and they were together in another life, and now they lived the result of a reincarnation.

In the last month of vacation, the two stealthily in secret, hidden behind an innocent lies, they met day after day sipping the nectar of the first love.

Eventually, the parents found out about the foam wave of love on which their children were floating.

The resistance of the parents has been in vain because after

Lucian graduated, the young people, willingly or without permission, they were married. Olguţa's parents remained with the satisfaction that Lucian Haimovici agreed to take wife's name, Hălăuceanu. At that time Lucian Hălăuceanu did not suspected that soon, after few years, this change of name would be useful to them.

A place of pharmacist, in the township of Pungeşti, for a young absolvent exceeded his expectations. The pharmacy was located in the absolute center of the township featuring also as a spacious home. It was surrounded by good shops in which you could find delicatessen Greek olives, Turkish sweets and other products for all tastes.

As in Roman, Olguţa shined in all occasions. Her upbringing, sociable, gregarious talkative person won fast the friendship of the other ladies in the township. Everyone knew the she was descended from an old wealthy family so they did not think that her husband would have Jewish blood. Among the intellectuals from Pungeşti Lucian, by his physical presence, but especially by his professional qualities was an agreeable person and respected. The amalgamation politic did not interest him, not even the legionary movement.

*

The transgressions committed by Legionary (the Iron Guard) rebellion culminated in the pogrom of 21-23 January and June, 1941, in Iassy, which caused terrible massacres, destruction, looting and disorder. King Michael I was neutral, he didn't mix with the legionaries and therefore, they skillfully tried to abstain not to bother knowing the tense relations between the king and general Antonescu.

On the eve of the rebellion, although the king was in Sinaia, a group of Iron Guard members were singing "Live the King" in front of the royal palace. On the day of rebellion the legionaries attempted to bring the king to Bucharest, but Antonescu turned them back to Sinaia.

The rebellion poured like a devastating hail over Jews with catastrophic effects that went beyond any imagination. It took place especially in Iassy and Bucharest. They have destroyed and robbed shops and houses, the owners were beaten, tortured and killed without mercy. Synagogues, schools and other Jewish monuments were set on fire, profaned and destroyed. Young legionary, with no pity, sadistic mutilated, killed with barbarism innocent people, just for the fact that they were Jews.

In Bucharest the rebellion began with a parade of the legionaries on Victory Avenue. Then they started the violence taking by assault, destroyed or arson the Jewish stores on communities like Văcăreşti, Dudeşti, the Rahova Street and other well-known addresses. They damaged and robbed also shops that belonged to Romanian, Italians, and Armenians. The legionnaires occupied by force the prefecture of police, the phones and the radio station Bucharest. he Jews were lifted from their homes then were taken and murdered in the forest of Băneasa or in the slaughterhouse from Străuleşti where they have been suspended to the hooks of the slaughterhouse.

A few of those from the lot that were shot in the forest Băneasa, because of cold, and lighter wounds, wake up after they passed out and found themselves in an image of nightmare. Dozens of naked corpses were lying on a carpet of bloody snow. The lucky survivors, dressed in tattered clothes have managed to reach Bucharest.

The armies intervened in force and reprimand the legionaries' aggression. The police headquarters has been released, the phones resumed its activity and the radio began to transmit, mostly news.

Legionnaires' headquarters on Roma Street has been riddled

with bullets. The strap of soldiers on Victoria Avenue and from other streets staid in alert until the rebellion has been dissolved. The next day on Victoria Avenue and toward the Arch of Triumph a column of motorized Germans passed in threatening force and big speed.

On the streets were burning candles in the memory of the dead soldiers, for which, later has been organized a military funeral.

In Iassy the situation became even more frightening. The streets have been turned into chaos. Young legionary, on the streets, or on open trucks were shouting, singing, laughing loudly, molesting or maltreating by passers. The shops have been broken and looted, monuments crumpled, and synagogues set on fire, hundreds of people were tortured and killed with bestiality; this is how it looked the beautiful capital of Moldavia.

Among the leaders of the anti-Semitic movement of Iassy was the Archbishop of Moldavia. He had forgotten too quickly, that he has been saved, some time ago, by the Jews. He participated in a political movement, showing a lot of weakness. When he was about to be apprehended and jailed, he found refuge in a synagogue, disguised as Rabbi. He stayed hidden until his friends have been able to cancel the order for his arrest and freeing him with clean face. But sometimes in life happens as in the well-known proverb: "The one who you don't let die will not let you live".

Under the pressure of the patriotic forces the legionary movement has been removed from power and prohibited.

Horia Sima who organized the rebellion, went into hiding. He suffered a nervous breakdown and tried to kill himself. He fled immediately to Germany having on him an invitation with the stamp from Gestapo. In Vienna he formed ghosts govern waiting to return to power.

Legionnaires have been scattered but the persecution against the Jews continued because Hitler had declared that "he wants a New Europe, without Jews".

*

On Sunday it was a day of fair in Pungeşti. From babies up to grandfathers, from peasants dressed in traditional pants and traditional sandals to the judges and lawyers with their shiny shoes, from the country women wearing natural flowers in their hair up to the fine ladies such as the wife of the pharmacist with her curled hair and silk dress, everyone, who could breath and walk was in the center of the fair or on the pavements. Some were setting up business, others came for fun, but all of them were talking politics, being touched by the rebellion that took place in January and the deportations of Jews. The musician groups from neighboring villages of Doagele or Porcăreţ were doing their own publicity trying to cheer up the spectators. Whatever they earned, most times, remained at the fair at the pubs.

The Jews did not care for music, they were retained trying not to ruin the good time of others.

Teodora and Dragomir came rarely on Sundays at the fair, but, now, it was really necessary. They understood Berta's and Isidor's desire and impatience to see their son; they couldn't see him for a whole week.

Teodora and Dragomir were also still marked by the tragedy of their child's death. Each gesture, whine or smile of Mihai reminded them of their child Mihai, whose body was buried in a foreign crypt. They waited and waited, that in time, their wounds will heal, because the time, in general, cures these kinds of wounds. Until then, for those around them, who did not know their drama, they tried, as much as they could, to adopt a normal behavior.

It passed seven days since their angel was strolling into heaven. On Saturday she prepared two baskets filled with all sort of goodies: one for church and another for their brothers Berta and Isidor.

Teodora, dressed in a cherry suit cherry, received from Berta, with silk stockings and shiny shoes was walking lithely, imitating the walk of a deer in the forest. With her black head kerchief she build sort of coronet knotted on the back. It could have been proper to wear mourning cloth, but under the circumstances, the black head kerchief was enough and Mihai, the one who left her, will understand. She let her blond hair freely, and discretely looked at Dragomir to capture his reactions. Her husband was enjoying seeing his wife taking care of herself, as in the good times.

Mihai was in a white suit, with boots and hat also white.

However, she placed a red ribbon on him, not to have someone scare the boy at the fair. It was beautifully their child. He grew up in seven days like the Prince Charming from the story with the same name. The forest's clean air and the sun gave him a new color. His cheeks caught the peonies color and his eyes took the shine of violets from the big meadow of God.

Dragomir, in new suit, looked younger. He didn't care much about his green bowler but he could not avoid wearing it being part of his Ranger uniform. He also shined well his weapon allowing it to be visible, but without being loaded. It never had happened to make use of it but any one with strange intensions stepped back when he saw the weapon. The baskets filled with many prepared goods by Teodora have been arranged on the back seat of the carriage on a new colored carpet with shades of green and natural beige.

First they stopped at the church, distributed, following the tradition, alms, pies and sweet breads, in the memory of their children Dumitru and Mihai.

People knew that their first child died, and so there was no doubt that would blame them in connection with their Christian ritual at the church.

With their souls at peace, they stopped at the front door of Isidor's shop. There was parked also the white car of doctor Manea from Vaslui. The newcomers shacked of emotion and worries thinking that something bad happened. "What if something bad happened with Berta or Isidor?" Their fear vanished when the two of them appeared in the door looking and smiling, with their eyes fixed on the child on Teodora's arms. As usual, the shop's doors have been locked, not to be disturbed. In the living room waiting, with open curiosity, were Iulia and Teodor Manea. They have been specially invited by Isidor. They shook hands warmly and with pleasure. Iulia hugged and kissed Teodora, this showed that she liked her from the first moment. Dragomir placed the basket in the kitchen, on the table. All were looking at Mihai as to a heavenly gift. The child dress in white from top to toes was looking as a little prince; this image made Berta and Isidor thinking alike: "If they would not have had to wait for their forced deportation, they would have taken the child back, forgetting all the pre-arrangements. Berta extended her arms towards Mihai to hug him. The child withdrew his face and kind of hides it near Teodora's face, sign that he doesn't want to go anywhere.

Teodora said kindly: "My darling, go! She is your mother ma-ma."
The child understood and extended his little arms towards who he
recognized. "Ma-ma", said Mihai for the first time the magic word.
All around him remained astonished by the unexpected gift offered by
the child. Berta and Isidor took turns in hugging the little angel,
enjoying the divine moments. Enchanted by so much love towards
him, Mihai extended his arms towards everyone who wanted to hug
him, laughing continuously. Iulia was someone he did not recognize
and he looked at her for a moment with curiosity. After this play back
and forth, the child wanted to Teodora's arms, who took him with
great love, intuitively guessing that he was hungry a little tired. She
placed him comfortably and offered her milk which he sucked with
pleasure until he fell asleep.   Teodora placed him on a couch,
knowing that he'll sleep for at least an hour, smiling in his sweet
dreams.

They sat at the table and eat from the good food prepared and
brought by Teodora. Doctor Manea, under a low voice started to share
the latest news he found out from Vaslui and Iași. On everyone faces
you could read the worries of uncertainty. Iulia and Teodor Manea
finished their visit and asked to be excused because they needed
leave. They were away from Vaslui for almost half a day and several
patients were waiting their return. Followed a series of compliments
and expressed their desire to see each other soon. Teodora invited
them all to get together next Sunday, at the Canton.

*

The known doctor Teodor Manea from Vaslui had his own history.

His parents Cecilia and Toader, although rich people, full of money, how some were thinking, were modest and wise people. For their unique child Teodor, the only thing they wanted was that he will get a good education, as much education as possible.

The boy grew up in this atmosphere imposed by his parents, and did not want to deceive them, especially that he liked to read and study a lot. Since his high school years, Teodor wanted to become a doctor. He became friend with a colleague, in high school, who was the daughter of the priest from Laza. She basically had the same goals as him. She was a beautiful and smart; Iulia was attractive also through her irresistible optimism.

Iulia's mother died at birth and her father did not re-marry. All his love and attention was directed to his daughter, who he venerated as a precious icon.

The priest from Laza was very well known as a special man, he was appreciated by his church parishioners as well as by his superiors. The episcopate of Huşi or of Roman made him several times the proposal to take a position at episcopate. The priest being very much connected with his parish took the decision to remain and serve in Laza.

Iulia grew up being guided by the principle of love for people, and, in general, for those who must, in conformity with the beings laws, to enjoy everything that the nature provided to us. She admired the grass, the flowers and most of all the trees, which she considered superior and example of dignity because they start, live, sleep, and die standing. For Iulia's future was destined a profession of doctor, that would fit her perfectly. She was dreaming since she was little that this will be what she wants to become when she'll grow up.

Iulia and Teodor left together to Iaşi at the Medicine University always they were seen together everywhere, at courses, at lunch, library or at the hospital.

When Teodor was in the third year of study, a great and unexpected pain and sufferance came into his life. His both parents died while in a cruise ship on a Danube river. In a night with a dense fog the ship, full of tourists, sank. There were no survivors.

In the first moment, when Teodor heard about this tragedy, had the sensation that himself is sinking. The fortune ran away from him without looking behind.

He understood for the first time that all major things have a double aspect, meeting on a boundary between good and bad, between white and black, between hate and love, between bitter and sweet, between wise and weakness, and to find the good avenue you must walk always with an open eye evaluating what you do and your power! Iulia helped him to select the white, the good, and the love, becoming his guiding star.

Until the time he lost his parents Teodor didn't know anything about his father Toader Manea business, who was a famous lawyer in Vaslui. About him there was circulating a tale: the lawyer was very solicited and when he was walking on the street, his client stopped and reminds him that the next day they'll have to meet at court house or at his office. Toader Manea had in in the small pocket of his jacket a small watch made of massive gold and the chain the same. At each of these types of encounters with a client he was changing the watch on the opposite pocket saying "Good thing you reminded me. Look I put the watch here, so I don't forget!" Fact is that the lawyer knew perfectly all his appointments, and the story with the watch was something that he was doing to show his consideration for the clients.

After this tragedy, Teodor decided that the parents' house should be transformed in a medical cabinet and he'll make modifications and additions for the living quarters. His uncle Ghiţă Manea who was an experienced constructor engaged himself to help his nephew. The money remained in the existing bank accounts, using from there only the necessary money for maintenance.

Next year Iulia and Teodor got married and the priest Andrei accepted to arrange the medical cabinet.

When Iulia and Teodor graduated from the University, Vaslui was the place where they would practice their profession.

In few years Iulia and Teodor became the best and the most sought doctors in the city with patients from the whole county.

The friendship between Manea and Isidor from Pungeşti started in their childhood. Isidor, the senior, the merchant, was Manea's client and their families, in time, became friends. The same happened with their children who were of the same age. Between them there were no secrets, only sentiments of sincere friendship.

*

Passed more than two hours and in Isidor's living room they discussed about various important events. At that time the most shocking thing was the national and European tragedy lived by the Jews under the oppression of Hitler.
The dinner ended, Iulia and Teodor Manea left and the rest were waiting for Mihai to wake up.

Their thinking was transmitted to the child's dream. He opened his big eyes and broke the silence with a big ma-ma. It was like this word slept with him, it was on his tongue waiting for the vocal cords to push them out when he awakened. All four went to him and he smiled at all of them. Berta took him first in her arms, then Isidor with tears in his eyes, gave him a tour of the room. "O, God" was Isidor thinking, "how much joy and happiness in the same time." Berta started to change his diapers. While she undressed the baby she kissed him everywhere, as she was seeing him for the first time. The child felt her love and caresses and laughs continuously while his mother and father tried to hold their tears.

Dressed with clean cloth, Mihai would have liked a portion of milk but Teodora tried to delay this by distracting his attention. Mihai was happy surrounded by all the attention and was laughing. "Travelers need to leave now" said Dragomir, preparing to leave. "We thank you and we're waiting next Sunday to see you at our home, as we established", said Teodora. "Yes, with great pleasure, will come with Manea's family" confirmed Isidor; followed the hugs and the good byes.

The store door opened and the Ranger's family jumped in their carriage. The basket brought by Teodora full of prepared food was returned full of other goodies from Isidor' shop.

They started slowly, because on Sunday the main street was full of people. Teodora dressed in her new suite, with her hair left down, looked good and different. Actually, a wife of a Ranger cannot be compared with a common wife. On Dragomir's face one could read a proud feeling when he looked at her. People who knew him saluted them and others who were closer to him stopped for a few moments to admire the baby. "Good thing that I put him a red ribbon; otherwise these people would have scared my little baby."

It started a new week. The Ranger worked in the forest, as usual, walking all day long and inspecting the forest. The house chores remained on Teodora's shoulders. Firstly, she started with a general cleaning of the house in preparation for the next Sunday visit. She wanted that the guests will be received in a clean house as a pharmacy. Isidor was not a problem, because they knew each other for a while, but Iulia and Manea were people known in the whole county and she wanted to receive them in a special manner.

Starting Monday, Teodora realized that she cannot accomplish everything she wanted alone. A lot of major and minor things overwhelmed her. The cow needed to be attended because she was the milk provider, then the poultry of all kinds used most of her time, which she wanted to rather spend attending to Mihai. The baby was growing and the amount of time for his care increased also. In his small bed, with proper protection, he tried to get up and stand. He fall every time, but he tried again and again calling repeatedly ma-ma, ma-ma. Teodora's heart was melting when he called her. The other Mihai didn't have the chance to say mama. To make Dragomir happy she answered back to him with da-ddy. Mihai was looking at her a little curious; he didn't know what's going on.

While struggling to clean and arrange things around she remembered Vasilica, their neighbor from Gârceni, her home village. She remained an old maid, and at her age of 30 she didn't think to marry, she considered that she was too old for that. In childhood she suffered of a difficult illness, probably poliomyelitis. After long treatments, basically offered by the village's old women's popular herbal medicine, she survived; only one of her legs didn't want to listen to her commands, and preferred to be dragged. In her youth she didn't have boyfriends, she didn't go with girls to dance. Nobody asked her hand, even if her parents weren't poor. She was clean, delicate and knew to keep a house in order; she distinguished herself through a natural intelligence.

When Dragomir arrived home from the forest, Teodora explained to him her idea. Dragomir accepted her proposal without comments. While Dragomir prepared the stronger cart, because through the potholes of the villages' roads, until Gârceni, the carriage wouldn't have resisted, Teodora dressed the boy in a blue outfit, making sure that the red bow is perched on top as well. She took some additional changes for the baby, and then she dressed herself. In one hour they reached Gârceni.

Teodora's parents were very happy to see them. They didn't see the baby since the baptism ceremony, and they noticed that the boy changed a little bit. They didn't imagine, though that this Mihai is another Mihai.

They went to Vasilica's house and made the proposal to Vasilica, and she agreed, to go with them. She prepared a summary luggage, eagerly waiting to go. She said to her parents, in passing, that she is not going to the end of the world, just to justify in a way her rush and instant decision to go to the canton, about which she heard only laudatory things.

While Teodora was talking to the parents, Dragomir was showing Mihai around the courtyard full of animals and poultry. "See, daddy, this is the turkey, the poultry's king". Then they carefully approached the noisy and aggressive geese, the yellow cheeks as the yolk of an egg, which were bathing in a large basin, closely guarded by two male geese. "What else do you want daddy to show to you?" The child raised his arms up, as he wanted to fly, and looking in his eyes said "da-ddy". Dragomir stopped breathing for a second, he was overwhelmed with emotion and he had the sensation that he flies with the boy in his arms. Dragomir kept for himself the news knowing that this word will be repeated again and again.

Shortly they left, so they will arrive home during the day light. Mihai was sleeping in his mother lap and close to the canton when he waked up and looked at Dragomir, with a large smile, repeated again "da-ddy" word. Teodora was surprised and Dragomir was in the ninth cloud of happiness. "Yes, da-ddy I heard you!"

Followed happy days for parents, who were delighted to hear for the first time in their life the words of mama and daddy pronounced by the child. When sometimes, over Mihai's face, in their imagination, overlapped the face of the other Mihai, they shake their heads coming back to reality.

The preparations for Sunday's visit were almost ready. Vasilica proved to be a skilled housekeeper because everything she did was perfect.

Saturday, around noon, Dragomir came home very troubled. The Jews from Pungeşti were deported to Vaslui.

Sunday, as it was established, Manea family came at the canton. It wasn't a day for a joyful reunion, but the promise had to be kept.

*

The Jews from Pungeşti have been evacuated according to the government order of evacuation and the Jews have been sent to the city of Vaslui. The decision was stipulating that in the first faze all Jews to be gathered in the urban centers, in the large cities.

The order was a hypocrite one. One thing was written and other things were done. These are several fragments from the document:

"To the Mayor and to the Notary of Pungeşti:

Conform to the order that came from our superiors measures should be taken to evacuate all Jew families from the rural communities of the county to its capital Vaslui. We ask you that along with the gendarmerie's help to start immediately the evacuation of the Jewish families and direct them to Vaslui.

The families that are evacuated will not be allowed to access their homes in which they lived; therefore they should pack the necessary things for living. The things left behind will remain in your care. Those who will be caught red handed will be sent to the Military Court of Justice and will be sanctioned with the death penalty. Also, will be punished extremely harsh all those who will prove to be incorrect during this discharge.

The measures that you'll take towards the evacuees should be civilized, and their feeding supplies will be in the care of the prefecture.

The evacuation operation will be performed immediately. You will be held responsible for the execution of this order."

The mayor of Pungeşti, kind man, and without green shirt had to obey and execute the order. Together with the office of gendarmerie requisitioned carts and in twenty-four hours the Jews, with just the bare necessities, were picked up and sent to Vaslui. The journey to Vaslui was long and column of evacuees made a pause at the famous Inn of Mitică Ioan. The gendarmes in charge of the column, entered into the inn to eat and even to drink a few glasses of wine. The Jews didn't have permission to leave the perimeter imposed. The owner was not a politician but a man, and he took some measures of common humanity. His helpers, at his orders brought to each Jew bread, cheese and biscuits. While outside the boys distributed food, inside the owner was keeping the gendarmes company talking and even giving them a glass of wine, free-of-charge. For the Jews the gesture of Mitică Ioan lit up for a moment their lives, giving them a shred of confidence.

When they reached Vaslui city they saw how quickly things changed like one changes white to black. Randomly they have been accommodated at residents' families or in vacated houses. Berta and Isidor were taken to some people at the outskirts of the city beyond the public garden.

The two of them got in touch with other friends from Vaslui and decided to go to Câmpulung, where was Berta's family. They didn't foresee that in a few months, the fate of those of Câmpulung will turn into a tragedy.

Paying lots of money, by bribing some influential people, the six Jews from Vaslui, with forged documents took the train to Câmpulung, sitting in different wagons. After a night of travel, exhausted of fear and sleeplessness, they arrived to the Berta's relatives who received them with love.

In the city it was the quiet as before the storm. In connection with Mihai, the opinions were divided. After rebellion and deportations that started, leaving your child in the care of some trusty friends of trust was considered the wisest solution. The desire to see their child was grinding them like a sleepless worm. They wrote a brief, encrypted message to Dr. Manea from Vaslui, waiting eagerly answers. The doctor responded to them, as if they were his own patients, giving them medical advice, inserting from place to place news about Mihai. "My nephew is well and this Sunday I've seen him", he wrote.

In short time started the war with the Russians, then started the pogrom of Iassy which worsened the Jews fate.

*

When the Jews departed from Pungeşti the marketplace changed. The shops, the stores and the banks were shut down with their shades pulled looking like some sinister masks.

The following Sunday people gathered in the center of the village being distressed and scared by the news they were hearing. With sad faces, people looked puzzled and could not believe that the shops were shuttered and the interiors empty. The news flew from man to man, some true, some exaggerated, but all having a kernel of truth. Marches, trains, mass deportations, Transnistria, Auschwitz and many others were carried on as by a cordless phone, frightening the world.

The decrees and laws against the Jews were produces as on a conveyor. First decree signed by Carol II was imposed to review the citizenship of Jews. Based on this decree, more than one third of the Jews of Romania have lost their citizenship. Immediately, followed the law on the legal status of the Jews, which among other things, stated that the mixed marriages were prohibited.

They have shut off the printings, translations and all Jewish publications.

Came then the elimination of doctors, teachers, judges from the institutions in which they worked. The intention was that by these measures will be created a big Romanian in culture and science.

Jews were forced to wear sewn on their jacket the yellow Star of David, which was a model borrowed from the German Nazism. Following the meeting between W. Filderman, president of the Union Jewish Communities in Romania, and I. Antonescu, the marshal cancels the order which has not been respected in some places. In Moldova, and Transnistria, Cernăuţi the Jews were forced to wear still the distinctive Star of David. In Transnistria (where it was named a Romanian governor) were made excessive and higher demands, the Jews being forced to mend on their clothing on the left-hand side of the chest next to the Star of David a serial number that they have received from authorities. They have imposed to Jews all sorts of restrictions. There were hotels, restaurants, hospitals, pharmacies in which Jews had no access. On the door of a pharmacy was writing: "The entry of Jews and of dogs not permitted". The Jews were forced to work different jobs for the benefits of the community.

An old man, who was a violinist at the Bucharest Philharmonic, was cleaning the snow on the streets with his hands frozen. In the face of this horrification, many Romanians took attitude offering tea and sandwiches to those forced to work in cold. Some owners decided to clean themselves the street.

Over the whole country was pouring black drops of dark gray ash. The occupation forces allied with the government, swarmed in an iron rope the shaky body of Romania, which did not yet enjoyed enough to the realization of the Great Unification from 1918.

The Romanian and German armies on the bank of Prut River were prepared to confront the Russians. For the liberation of Bessarabia and Northern Bukovina the Romanian army was ready to redden with their blood the crashing waters of the river.

The order to attack has been given by general I. Antonescu in the morning of 22 June 1941 and it had the following content: "Soldiers, I command: Go cross the Prut River! Crush the enemy from the east! Free from Bolshevism our occupied brothers! Reintegrate the Country's body and, its woodlands, the fertile land of Basarabian from Bukovina. Soldiers! Let's go on to victory road of Stephen the Great and conquer the ancestor's land. Be proud of the Romanian past!"

On the radio, along with the I. Antonescu discourse the bells of the big Cathedral from Chisinau rang.

The decision to cross the river Prut belongs to I. Antonescu. The King Mihai learned about Romanian entry into the war from the British radio station, B.B.C.

It was Sunday morning 29 June 1941, when the streets of Iassy were full of policemen, gendarmes, Romanian and German soldiers who have removed by force the Jews from their homes on the street and batted and gunned down, immediately those who dared to resist.

Those who have received information from their Romanian friends, about a pogrom being prepared, have fled, they hid manage to escape with their life. A few months before, Antonescu had ordered that the Jews in rural localities, near battlefield and in the war areas, to be moved to the big cities.

At the time of the pogrom in Iassy were about forty thousand Jews, local people and evacuees. Initially, it started with a maneuver, calling the Jews, calmly, at the police station for the verification of their documents. Some of them have received a voucher stamped with "free", and let go home. Those who remained at the station, under various pretexts, had a barbaric treatment. Seeing that the authorities do not intervene to the organizers of the pogrom has caused an outrage upheaval against the Jews. There are no words that can describe the cruelty with which they have treated and murdered the Jews in the back yard of police quarters. The dead were thrown into mass graves dug in Jewish cemetery of Iassy. There were people who died with their eyes removed, tongs, ears and arms cut, hanged on the gallows in the slaughter houses, in a terrible anguish and nobody could do anything to save them.

The pogrom of Iassy was the worst massacre from the whole Romanian territory. Within a few hours, the police courtyard degenerated into a corner of hell, which was brought on the earth. The Jews taken from their homes or from the street, without reason, realized that the situation that they had lived during the rebellion, repeats in a form much more serious. Heat and the exposure to the sun contributed to a fast deterioration of the children whose tears on their cheeks were drying, waiting for some relief.

On the night of June 29, many Jews families were taken from their homes, carried outside of town and executed. Isac, a child, lucky survivor, will tell you later what he did to escape death.

*

The group in which was Isac, started on a secondary road of the county, toward a forest. From the discussion of the leaders of the group, it was retained the word Popricani. Later, it has been found a common grave at Popricani, where the murdered Jews have been buried.

The soldiers and gendarmes, with batons, horse whips and weapons, were on the horseback, making fun of those who were unable to walk due to thirst, hunger and fatigue. Those who could not rise after falling were gun down on the spot.

When the group entered in the Popricani forest the sun was getting ready to step over the treetops and a dense shadow fall over them providing, for a moment, some relief.

A father was shaking his boy of three years by placing him on his shoulders to relieve his fatigue and crying. One of the two German soldiers, pretending that he didn't understand the paternal gesture, took it as a provocation and shut the little boy in the head. The blood with his brain tissue, pieces of flesh and bone spattered all around them, causing indignation and a wave of shouts echoed through the forest. The bustle produced, had led to screams of terror and shoots that shuddered Isac, urging him to take a risky decision. The child hided at the very root of a tree beside him faked conscious or not, a passed out state. Lying on his back, his eyes closed, he was waiting for the verdict's fate.

Listening with attention, he noticed that the noise of the group faded away but he dared not to open his eyelids. An object small and tough, hit him right in the forehead, making him jump up. Bullet could not be, as long as he still has his head. Slowly he opened his eyes, and saw on a small branch, actually above his head a squirrel collecting walnuts. Then, with a jump, the little creature was next to him. It was like a sign from Heaven.

The squirrel started jumping through the herbs and shrubs, as though urging him to follow. Isac rose, he was frightened, but seeing nobody around decided to follow the little creature. The direction in which they walked was vice versa, the path by which the convoy passed.

After an hour of running, the squirrel stopped near an eye of water, clear and bright. In the middle of this pond it was a small stream coming up from under the ground. Isac being terrible thirsty jumped and drank from the heavenly water and then cleaned his cheeks, forehead and hair.

The squirrel, with a jump, without a ladder, climbed an old oak looking the boy into his eyes. The child understood the message: it was growing dark, and he had to sleep. He sat, at the root of the tree. Soon the hum subsided, only the count endlessly buzzes of the crickets could be heard. Through the grasses he could see here and there sparks jumping. The child, frightened remembered, however, that all the tiny insects photo-luminescent were, in fact the fireflies. He was safe.

He wakened up caressed by a concert of birds which he had never heard before, wondering if he's still alive or has been shot, as the poor little toddler, and now is in Heaven. The squirrel, the spring, fireflies, the concert there were too many, for a condemned to death. He rose to his feet and looked at the golden frame, which neatly trimmed the tops of the trees from the east side. The squirrel came close to him and jumped as she was ready to guide him. After a few jumps it stopped beside some bushes, full of red raspberries and blueberries covered by the morning dampness. The hungry boy started to picked the fruits with both hands and eat them without chewing. When he felt that he had enough made a sign to the squirrel that he's ready.

The sun was up when the two runners emerged from the forest. A dusty road separated the forest from the fields of ripen wheat almost ready for harvest. The squirrel jumped along the road for a while and then stopped, looked for a couple of moments the child in the eyes, raised one of his paws and shake and then started to jump back from where they came. "Don't leave, squirrel! Do not leave me!" But his begging was in van. The squirrel disappeared from his view like she entered into the ground, leaving him to make his own decisions.

Maturity exam came too soon for the little boy, and he suddenly felt that the gates of his mind opened giving him courage. He remembered that he has an uncle at Târgu Neamț.

He saw a wagon, with camping gypsies projecting on the horizon, coming in his direction, where the squirrel left him. When the wagon reached him, Isac waved at the coachman. The coachman with long hair combed smoothly, a black brimmed large hat and slyly pants of velvet, slightly discolored, stopped asking where he goes.

"At Târgu Neamț," answered the child, very precisely.

"It's quiet far, and we'll only go up to Roman, but come on, get on wagon. Without hesitation, Isac climbed, saying, "Good day". There was no answer and a gypsy woman, probably the wife coachman, motioned to him to sit down between two boys, about his age. The woman was beautiful; wearing a chain of fake gold coins asked him what is his name. "Aurel" quickly he said, and was very glad that came up with a name. Under the tilt of the wagon, in the shade, Aurel felt like in a family. They all ate all from black bread, drinking water from the same jug.

They went to Roman, bypassing the city, on a side road. At the edge of a small forest of acacia alongside of the road they stopped at a gypsy camp around a large fire, with reddish flames and hot charcoals. Haralamb's wagon aligned up near other wagons. They all knew each other. The children jumped in order from the wagon, shaking their bodies and extremities.

In just a few seconds, some large copper pots filled with meat have been placed on the red charcoal. On a patch of grass, in the shade, the women were laying on the ground a huge flowery fabric cloth as their head kerchiefs. Five large loafs of bread, have been broken with the hands by the women, in equal pieces, as though it would be weighed.

The children, including Aurel, received metal plates which were used as drums while waiting for the stakes.

The men took careful care of the steaks on the pans, talking loud and with large gestures expressing their indignation and outrage to the inhuman measures of the government. Aurel, pretending that plays with the plate, actually was eavesdropping, striving to retain what they talk about.

"I've heard from a Romanian citizen in confidence", said one that "Antonescu will send us to Bug. This friend of mine, advised me that I must be going in the mountains, in a village with Romanized gypsy, get read of our wagons, and live in houses, like everyone else. I suggest to you all to set ourselves in a village."

Others gypsy men scratched their beards, asking, without a word, reflection time.

The steaks were giving off an irresistible smell, sign that they are done, and the children with the plates in hand, formed a queue: The small ones in the front helped by the girls, followed by the rest of the children in order of their age.

The men took the large pans from the heat, handing them to the women to make the distribution. The food was plenty and they all got the portions in silence. The women, girls and the small ones were sitting together in the same place. The older boys had their gang, including Aurel. The men had kept their places near the fire and with the food in their hand, continued their discussions.

"But this one, where did you fish it?" asked one man, "He is not one of us."

"It's an orphan child", said Haralamb, "He goes to Târgu Neamţ, to his grandparents."

Finally, after long discussions it was decided that all will go to Târgu Neamţ. At sun set the whole group quiet down going to sleep. The women and children slept in the wagons squeezed one near the other like canned sardines. The men and big boys older than twelve years prepared their sleeping places under the carts. The horses, tied on the carts, eat all night long their oats, enjoying the clean air of the forest.

After a good and sound night's sleep and stout, when the stars began to fade away on the sky, the horses have been harnessed and the wagons started to move on the road, on a cool morning. Aurel woke up in the shaking of the cart, but seeing that the other children, who were used with this rocking of the cart, were still sleeping, closed himself the eyes.

Toward noon they have reached the edge of the township, and the carts stopped on a bare patch, well walked over, probably, especially reserved for stopovers.

"Hey, boy, this is Târgu Neamţ" said Haralamb.

Aurel, smiled at them all, thanking them for hospitality and start to walk on a large street that led toward the center of the township.

The child was surprised to see that also in Târgu Neamţ were many small shops closed. He asked a few handicrafts, if they know where Mr. Iancu lives, but the answers were the same: "Which Iancu?" perhaps, Isac though, there were more than one merchant with the name of Iancu, but a different name he didn't know. It occurred to him to ask about the synagogue which he discovered immediately. The door of the synagogue was closed and the child sat down leaning his back against the cool wall. He was dozing, when a few steps away from him, he saw an old man with a white beard approaching the door. Isac stood up on his feet, greeting the old man, who seemed to be the Rabin.

"I'm looking for Mr. Iancu, my uncle, said the little child with a faded voice.

The Rabbi, at-a-glance realized that in front of him was a Jewish child without parents and family. He just found out about the pogrom from Iassy, the crimes from the Popricani's forest and from the Vulturi's forest.

Gently, the Rabbi made Isac to tell where he comes from and how he managed to escape. In the town there have been three merchants with the name of Iancu, but all have been deported. The child should not know yet the truth. Rabbi invited him at his home, until they'll find his uncle Iancu.

The largest group that remained in the yard of the Superintendent has been taken to the station and embarked on the so called "train of death", with the direction Călăraşi. The trains were freight wagons old and dirty, with the doors and windows covered with wooden planks, which moved very slow, as a snail, stopping for hours on minor stations.

A train which started in Iassy arrived at the Ilioaia's Bridge after a whole day. Without food, water and air, on an unbearable heat, people were dying at a high rate.

The dead bodies have been buried into mass graves, wherever the train stopped along the rail road. The trains of death were used all over the country. Some came from Bulgaria or Greece heading to the death camps in Poland.

In the train stations where they stopped, instead of water or food the Jews were subjected to the most terrible humiliations and anguish. Young people, who wear their green shirts along with other violent fools, eager for sadistic thrills, boarded the trains humiliating the condemned without blame or throwing them of the window like bags.

*

When they left Vaslui in the direction of Iassy, doctors Iulia and Teodor Manea didn't foresee any surprises on that bloody day of Sunday 29 June.

They had lived with pain, and fear the rebellion days, then the changes and governmental decrees against the Jews, but always hoping that one day all this nonsense will end. But wasn't so, on the contrary.

They intended to reach Iassy to bring home Radu, their friend, who was for a long time under treatment, at the Hospital "Saint Spiridon". As soon as they crossed the Red Bridge an unusual bustle inspired them concern and even fear. On the streets located between Mitropolie and Bahlui hundreds of people, especially men, were walking in messy columns toward the police headquarters.

Young hooligans, gendarmes, Romanian and German soldiers vandalized the deported Jewish houses, pulling out by force the people from their homes and forcing them with brutal and rude arguments to get into column.

Dr. Manea had the impression that he was standing in front of a rebellion. The street of Ştefan the Great could not be used with the car. They went around the city bypassing the center of the city, and following the tram line to a Cuckoo'sTârg and then turned left to the hospital. A cop checked their documents, and finding that they are doctors let them pass with a special permit.

In the hospital nobody knew about the pogrom, even though they had a couple of wounded who have been brought in, but they didn't divulge anything, it was like their mouths were sewn. Dr. Manea could not go indifferently over these very serious events and entering into the cabinet of a colleague, found the actual situation: The city of Iassy is again under the pressure of the legionnaires although they were no longer in power.

Iulia did not enter in the hospital, preferring to follow, on the stairs, the turmoil of the street. Her attention was attracted by a woman, with a basket in her hand, which entered into hospital's yard; she looked scared in all directions, as though eyeing for a hiding place. Spotting Iulia, the woman started to shake and putting quickly the basket next to the doctor's car, ran away in the market. Iulia came down stairs in a hurry toward the basket left by the woman. In the basket was a baby sleeping. At his feet was the bottle of milk and an illegible note: "Ana. Thank you very much".

Iulia realized that the little girl was the child of a desperate mother who left her in the hands of destiny. She believed that the woman who left the basket there was the desperate mother. But as there was no time for questions or research Iulia put the basket on the back seat listening carefully to the pulse, and respiration of the child, making sure that everything is normal.

Just then the doctor Manea and Radu approached the car. Iulia made a discreet sign to her husband and began with an explanation: "Radu, in the car we have also a passenger. It is the child of a woman in my father's parish that was admitted for treatment here, and now we are taking her home."

The two didn't comment. Iulia told them that she should get few things from the market, and do some small shopping.

At the market, she looked around carefully until she saw the woman with the yellow kerchief who abandoned the basket next to the car. She stopped next to her, and with a warm voice, not to scare her off; she asked "what is it with the little girl in the basket".

When she heard being asked so directly about the baby, she confessed the truth. The basket had been left by a woman in the Jewish convoy that was taken to the police headquarters. She took the basket, covered with kerchief, thinking that there was food. When she discovered that there was a child, she got scared, but she couldn't leave the basket in the street and decided to take it to the hospital, so that it would be safe.

"I am poor", said the woman and started to cry. "I don't have with what to raise one more child." Iulia gave her a few hundred lei, asking what her name is. "Anica Olaru, but please do not send me to the police because I have no guilt." "Stay calm, I didn't ask you for that, if you find out who are the parents of this girl, please let me know, I will reward you for that. My name is Iulia and I am doctor at the hospital in Vaslui. Thank you and good bye".

Iulia rushed away, pausing at the corner shop, from where she bought a pack of diapers, several cloths, and other small things for a baby girl. She arrived at the car loaded; the two men were waiting and worried.

The road back through Iassy became more difficult, because the turmoil from its center increased and took over the whole city. The driving became a little more normal after they passed the Bucium Hill. Being Sunday, the villages through which they passed, far away from the urban events, were enjoying the day of rest.

In Vaslui, they left Radu at his home, and then the car continued the road toward the canton, as Iulia decided. Now, on the way to the canton, the doctor found out from Iulia, the story about Ana. The girl's sleep was worrying, it seemed unnatural, but they suspected that her mother gave her a sedative with an extended effect.

They reached the canton. In front of the gates locked Manea honked slowly. Dragomir and Teodora were at home, and were happy to see the doctors. When they heard the scope of their visit, they felt flattered because of the trust shown by the doctors.

The only favor the doctors asked was that Vasilica and other people to know that the girl is Manea's family.

In the house, they put the little girl in the large bed. They undressed her and gave her a detailed checkup. They turned her on all sides, washed and dressed her, but Ana continued to sleep. The doctors were convinced that the sleep is due to a sedative and the parents didn't seem to worry about it.

Mihai was sleeping also in his bed, perhaps even dreaming that he has a little sister.

After a while, Ana began to move her body extending her joints. She opened her eyes and unrecognizing anything around her she started to cry. She cried with big, clear tears of a scared baby. Teodora, without asking the consent of the doctors, took the girl and offered her the breast. The girl's tears miraculously stopped. She sucked staring into Teodora's eyes. They probably didn't much her mother's but the milk was good.

When Mihai woke up he received his portion of milk on the other breast. Then they introduced the two children to each other. The girl was skinny, but with a surprising energy and her look was powerful that passed through the man. Dressed in a pink suit she looked as a rose bud on the move. Mihai was looking at her being attracted by the pink color basically. Placed besides each other they looked as a pair of children from a fashion magazine for children. In Mihai's small bed, the children attempted to hug each other thinking, maybe, that the other is himself in other color outfit. They touched each other's cheeks. Mihai wanted to reach Anna's eyes with his index finger. She reacted closing her eyes without any reciprocated gesture.

Iulia and Teodora were walking with the children in their arms through the gates of the canton, in the forest. The men behind were speaking expressing to each other their concern about the Jews pogrom.

Ana, probably, didn't ever saw a forest; she wanted to reach each leaf that was touching her forehead. Mihai was talkative showing his superiority by repeating like a parrot, "ma-ma", "da-ddy". Ana didn't pronounce any word and looked curiously at the little boy.

They stopped under the fowler's pear or the true service tree, which was unique in the forest a kind of axis moundi, the patriarch of the forest. The Ranger Gherasim who built the canton found it there, young, and of an average height. In a few decades the fowler's pear grew continuously, increasing his crown and went with its roots deep in the black soil like metal anchors. Who knows which miraculous bird brought the seed in its beak in this place? Although in each fall thousands of pears fell, on the same earth, none of them was able to catch up and sprout. Nature has blessed it without followers. The old fowler's tree, selfish shall enjoy all the benefits. All by-passers admired it. Some stopped to relax at its shadow and the forests' birds gathered on its majestic branched crown as for a religious ceremony. This tree was the Lord of the forest and a marking point.

Slowly, slowly they started to return home, the babies in women arms were tiered and almost falling asleep.

Home, they put them on the big bed near one another. The parents sat at the table on the veranda. Vasilica didn't know the current unhappy events up to date that, and decorated the house and the table very festively. She was surprised that the guests weren't too joyful, but didn't dare to ask anything.

The good food, especially prepared by Teodora was just tasted. Everyone lost their appetite, and all were thinking at the Isidor and Berta's whereabouts.

To change the thoughts, doctor Manea came up with a proposal. "We, probably we'll adopt Ana; but because we don't know her date of birth we thought to put the same date of birth as that of Mihai: ten January one thousand nine hundred and forty-one.

"How nice from your part," said joyfully Teodora. At Teodora's insistence, Ana remained for a couple of months at the canton, away from the lightning of war and the pogrom against the Jews.

*

The East frontline advanced very fast. After almost two week of fights, the city Cernăuți was liberated. The liberation of the North of Bukovina was the first success. It followed then the liberation of the city of Bălți, and Soroca town. By the end of the month of July the whole Romanian occupied territory has been liberated.

The commander of the Romanian-German front issued the following communicate: "The fight for the liberation of the Romanian land from the East is finished. From the Carpathian Mountains to the Sea we are again the owners of our forefathers land." King Mihai, accompanied by I. Antonescu made in July a visit on the battlefield and to the city of Cernăuți. The King refused, later on, to visit Odessa and Transnistria.

When it came the time to force the Nistru River, the Romanian army and the officers became demoralized, uncomprehendingly why the battle continued when the Romanian land was liberated.

They didn't know that at the beginning of the month of June, at Munich was signed a Romanian-German agreement by which the government led by Antonescu was forced to participate until the end in the war against U.S.S.R.

In August, I. Antonescu was promoted to the position of marshal. Romanian army already had other two marshals, nominated by Carol II: Constantin Prezan and Alexandru Averescu.

The marshal Alexandru Averescu, dedicated member of a literary group "Junimea", was enjoying the respect of the literati and philosophers of those times. The King considered him among personalities at the time along with the Nicolae Iorga.

The political enemies have tried to liquidate him by organizing a complot with bombs. But the marshal escapes alive.

In September, 1941, the frontline was already near the border of Odessa. Heavy fighting took place at Țiganca, where more than one thousands Romanian solders lost their lives, being buried in mass graves near the village Epureni.

After the war, in the village took place exhumations have and priests held sermons in the memory of those fallen. A wooden gate sculpted in Maramureș and a cross watches over the crosses and graves of the heroes.

The defeat of Odessa wasn't easy. It was September and the rain would not stop. The cold entered into solders' bones, all tired and hungry were marching down the fields and lateral roads because the main roads were mined. The nearest hospital was in Tiraspol. Ambulances hidden behind the first lines were continuously carrying the wounded. Most of them, very badly wounded, didn't even arrive alive at the hospital. The dead were buried on the battle field and their bones whiten by time can be seen even today scattered on those places.

In the month of October Odessa was conquered. At short time the Romanian military headquarters just installed in the city was bombed and destroyed.

Antonescu gave the order that one in every 100 people to be executed for each Romanian officer killed. A wise Romanian general, who had fought before in the First World War, assumed the responsibility of canceling the order given by Antonescu. Other acts of violence continued to be executed. In Odessa the Jews have been pulled from the city and sent to Dalnic following that night, in secret, to be executed. They were accused of collaboration, through certain methods with the Russians. A similar situation is to be repeated in the case of Romania, when the bombardments began the Jews being still blamed wrongly, that they have signaled to the English and American airplanes.

Grouped in campus, a bucket of gasoline has been pored over them and set on fire, the Jews were burned alive. Some of them were hanged on the streets or in public squares.

The year of 1941 has been disastrous for Romania. England declared war to Romania, same did Canada, Australia, South Africa, the U.S. and other countries allied with England.

The Germans didn't have too many supplies of gasoline and food even if the city of Ploieşti was at their disposal. A German officer in a conversation made the following statement: "In Romania the milk, honey, and oil are flowing." The Germans wanted at any cost to conquer Moscow, their grand trophy. The battles near Moscow lasted a couple of months finishing in April 1942 with defeat of the allied armies, which marked the beginning of decline of Hitler.

*

In the whole country took place massive concentration: all apt men and young were mobilized on the spot, receiving orders to enroll.

Such an order received also Dragomir Simionescu. The order of concentration came as a thunder over the Dragomir's family. Dragomir Simionescu was to join in twenty-four hours the 24th Infantry regiment from Vaslui.

He had to think fast what urgent measures to take that Teodora and Mihai will remain protected.

The first trip he made was at his father, former ranger. He had to move to canton, if Teodora would want to continue to leave there. Then, with the horse in foams, in an hour over the hills, he was at Gârceni to his in-laws and asked them to come the next day to canton. And for them, the news that Dragomir was concentrated came as an arrow.

Returned at home the ranger didn't know how to calm down his wife. Between the two of them there could be no more words but only tears. Mihai, although in his father's arms, seeing his parents crying began to whimper, anxious and agitated.

When the old man ranger, the father of Dragomir, who recently became pensioner, came to canton, the horse was already prepared ready to go. Dragomir must go to his brother Ioan Simionescu, brigadier in Brodoc. When his father, Gherasim became pensioner, Ioan became the head of the family the oldest among brothers. In Brodoc, Dragomir arrived in the middle of the night scaring all of them. When he told him what it is all about, the brigadier understood and tried to console him if there was room for such a thing..

Ileana, the wife of Ioan, intervened into discussions assuring her brother in law that they will take care of Teodora. Then he revealed the secret: Teodora was pregnant.

They left the horse in Ioan's stables and the two brothers left to Vaslui with Ioan's carriage. Woke up in middle of the night doctor Manea thought that something very grave happened to Mihai or Teodora. He felt better a little bit because the news brought by Dragomir was not great news but he didn't have seriousness of a fact thought by the doctor.

The doctor assured Dragomir that the next day together with Iulia would leave for canton. Because they'll go with the car, the doctor invited the brigadier to come with them. In this way the ranger left to the regiment somewhat at peace. His brother accompanied him until the gate where four soldiers were taking them into custody. The new enrollees were angry and unwilling.

Teodora couldn't sleep all night long. She was waiting for a better day to subdue her grief and to clear her thoughts. She didn't have any idea how many good people will be around her and how knew Dragomir, in so short a time, to take care of his family.

A sun of a late spring, which went long ago over the top of the trees which protected the canton, at sunrise, was smiling trying to spray with light the hearts worried of the fate of those going to the battlefield.

The yard was filled with relatives who came to encourage Teodora. The canton was the state's property, and at any time could come another ranger, with his family because the forest could not be left unattended, not even during the war.

Doctor Manea knowing more about Teodora and Mihai history felt somewhat responsible. The suspicious deaths of Teodora's two children were antecedents which had to be taken into consideration. Could be the case of a hidden disease, and because Teodora was pregnant, careful attention and prudence was required. Teodora felt some sort of undisclosed fear, preferring to listen to the two doctors.

Finally, the solution proposed by Manea, to purchase a house in Vaslui was supported by some, and disapproved by others. But Teodora's judgment became law and Manea's family offered to search for a home affordable, as she wished.

Every other day the doctors were coming at the canton bathing their eyes, and filling their lungs with the fresh air of the forest. Every time they brought with them Ana, their adopted girl. Iulia had a secret plan for Teodora to whom she always brought medical books, and pamphlets, asking her to look them over, and to keep her away from bad thoughts.

The forest was like a corner of Heaven in full effervescence, had become a true symphony of songs and colors. It was something that only in the biblical descriptions can be found.

While Ana and Mihai played under Vasilica's supervision, the mothers were discussing some of the items read by Teodora on the magazines received. Iulia attempted a sort of test on Teodora, and she was very happy that Teodora understood the material.

Teodora didn't sense what the doctors' intensions were, but being ambitious by nature, she sincerely wanted to be able to converse with Iulia on the medical issues. She had a good memory, which made Iulia believe that her plan will succeed.

Several times Teodora insisted that Ana remain at the canton to play with Mihai, but her parents could not be separated from the child who pampers them with her young brightness and kindness.

In Vaslui, as in other localities, the Jewish properties have been put automatically under the mayoral supervision and many wealthy people from the surrounding villages, who were interested to get them or to buy them. Will these properties bring them luck?

The evacuation of Jews touched Teodora very much, and she didn't want anything to do in this matter. She didn't want a house from where the Jews in tears left forced on unknown places. The luck was on her side because doctor Manea found a house exactly how Teodora wanted. The house had a garden and yard, being right next to the medical cabinet "Iulia and Teodor Manea".

The young man who was selling the house just returned from Paris and wanted to relocate to the capital. The house was empty for two years since the owners died, but a careful eye could see that the house had potential; the thick walls did not suffer during the earthquake of 1940 and all the damage was superficial. The war, still in full swing, had the prices fallen, especially of the houses. The young man, when at last found a buyer, asked for an affordable price and a barging would have been unnecessary.

The money left by Isidor was sufficient to cover the amount requested by the seller.

Manea took care of the buy/sell documents using his relations.

The whole family gathered and in very short time, about a month, the house was ready to move in.

The wood has been brought from the forests of Brodoc and Bălței purchased at the official price. The carpenters were young apprentices and professionals from the renowned carpentry of Aron's of Pungești. They were older people or very young who were exempt from the concentration.

They used their manpower of people from Gârceni.

The painters from Vaslui have been selected by recommendations.

The old furniture, of a remarkable value, has been repaired, and polished to be restored to the new condition..

The house was painted in white at Teodora and Iulia request.

The inside the arrangement of the rooms has been preserved, because the old owners were distinguished scholars: he was a lawyer, and she a teacher.

The fences and the gates were in good condition, and a fresh layer of paint, light brown, made them to harmoniously integrate with the house.

The garden, under Teodora's directions has been cleaned and restored to its initial design, maintaining its natural form as a patch of forest. The perennial unattended stubbornly lived following their natural cycle. The chrysanthemums bushes bloomed every year not taking into consideration the grasses that wanted to take over the garden.

When Teodora, Mihai and Vasilica moved to the new more comfortable place than the canton, they cried dearly when they left their loved forest, the source of health.

Teodora brought along her icons, the mirror received as a gift from Berta, Mihai's crib, their wedding gifts from the parents and cloth. For the treasure received from Isidor they found a new safe place, known only by her, and Manea family.

Father Andrei made the traditional asperges sprinkling the house with holy water, the same thing for the annexes, the draw well, the garden, the fences and the gate.

The next day the garden renews itself. The grass, flowers, trees sprinkled generously with water smiled satisfied in the sun of June. The garden was far from the corner of Heaven in the forest but responded to a large extent the expectations of the new owners.

On the first night Teodora began crying helpless thinking of Dragomir. The following night the same.

Mihai, too little to understand the vicissitudes of life, was a happy child. All day, under Vasilica's supervision, he played in the garden. He tried to walk, but was falling, and then he got up and fall again tripping on the disobedient herbs and grasses. When he fell first time, inside the house and hit his nose, he got scared so badly that cried. But he learned quickly to keep always the head up.

The child, amazed by the novelty of the landscape forgot quickly about the forest marvel. Teodora did not. The forest was indestructible connected to her love for Dragomir. She fell in love with him at seventeen when she went for the first time at the village dancing reunion. Many young girls in the village liked the lad even making advances to him, but he had eyes only for Teodora. When he finished the school of ranger, the two were married. The weeding was done with a big fast because Dragomir was the last, the youngest son of the ranger Gherasim. Together they were the ideal pair. But what a pity! The two children died when they were six months and Dragomir, when he thought that finally all these problems ended, had to go to war.

*

The old ranger Gherasim was retired, but after Dragomir left he was thinking how to protect Teodora and Mihai. Vasilica had become part of the family working hard to please everyone. Teodora was like her sister and Mihai was a marvelous child. The canton being located in the forest, a man with a gun was needed to protect the peace of the family; therefore, the presence of the old Gherasim was indispensable.

The first night, spent at canton, it had been for Teodora's father-in-law, a good adviser. The next day the call of the forest gave him an idea that nestled in his mind.

He dressed in the suit of ranger of his son, and told his Daughter-in-Law that he goes to see the forest. In fact taking the horse went directly to the Forestry Department located in Fâstâci. The department head knew him very well and was happy to see him again. He knew that the current ranger Dragomir was sent to war and didn't know who he should send there as substitute because almost all rangers have been mobilized. After Gherasim proposal to substitute his son until he comes back, the two of them convened that this was a good proposal. Gherasim was only sixty-five years old and could very well take his son's place until further notice.

In the evening, Gherasim came home with the order of appointment as ranger to substitute Dragomir. This was a relief for Teodora.

Becoming again the ranger of this forest, coming back after so many years to the canton built by himself before the First World War, the retired ranger had the feeling of floating above the reality.

The ranger had lived a life mixed with happiness and misery. He had dreamed palaces of crystal, had seen ferries swirling in his head, and patient but not defeated, at old age he lived alone.

In the early twentieth-century he had just finished the ranger's school. In two years he built the forestry canton on a place chosen by him: A round plateau, with forest all around made of oaks, linden and beech trees, that passed the century. The maple trees, corneal tree, and hazel trees sprouted there were they could find a free spot, being satisfied just with a few rays between the large crowns of the big, veteran threes of the forest. More recently, he planted on the abrupt part patches of acacia, knowing that their strong roots would stop the ground erosion and the sliding of the terrain. The wind and the birds spread over the fertile earth all kind of seeds that sprouted becoming flowering spreading all over.

The forest, literally, swarmed with all sorts of animals specific to the zone: hungry wolves, sly foxes, gracious deer and above all rabbits scared even of their shadow.

From time to time appeared a family of feral pigs, but they went on their way.

The canton was built with money from the state budget after Gherasim plans: four rooms, hallways, vestibules, the summer kitchen, stockyard, cages and other smaller places. The towering fences, with massive gates, surrounded the house, which become a real fortress. The canton became a point of reference for the roads that intersected there, as it was an Inn.

When all the work at the canton finished, the ranger who approached thirty years didn't want to leave alone and decided to marry. He didn't have hard time to find a wife, because any young lady wanted to become the wife of a ranger. At Easter, when he went at the dance festival in Valea Hogii, Gherasim set his eyes on a young, full of life, beautiful lady. The forester fell in love and in the fall they married.

Ileana his wife, who was much younger than him, got quickly used with the place and the customs of the house. In a couple of years the ranger's house became full with four lovely boys. Gherasim didn't have any problems: the house was good, the food plenty, the boys grew in the same way as the forest around them. He had also money because the trees were never counted! There were thunders, others broke due to the wait of snow, the storms uprooted some of the old oaks, so one tree next to another, and he could make some extra money besides his stipend.

All was good until one day when Ileana's heart was set on fire, falling in love with another man, the merchant Nicolae, a good friend of the family.

Sometimes the love is more powerful than rational; the two lovers have fled in the world, leaving behind their families.

Gherasim felt that he started with the wrong foot in his life, and kept on walking still with the left foot. He re-married twice, but both wives died relatively young, and then the ranger thought that the luck is too little, and out there are too many people waiting for it. He had four good children who filled his soul with joy and pride.

The return to the canton determined by reason of an emergency could be a lucky gift or a temptation.

*

Teodora got fast used with the life in the big city. Each day she took her child to go for a walk in fresh air. Mihai was very talkative; he had a question for everything, and asked for clarification keeping Teodora busy. He liked to be caressed, but most of all to be kissed. If Teodora didn't kiss him for a while, he was checking her face with his lips to attract her attention. When she put him in his bed to sleep, she was reading to him mostly everything, even medical magazines, and Mihai was listening with interest, even if he didn't understand anything.

One day Iulia took Teodora to their medical cabinet and proposed to her to work together. Then she told her what plans she prepared for her, and the fact that she was watching her for a couple of months to see her interest in medicine. She wished that Teodora become a medical assistant. Teodora learned very fast how to treat some patients, how to give a shut, how to assist the births or surgeries.

In the city, at the hospital, the wounded were arriving daily from the eastern front requiring long-term treatments. Ambulatory hospitals on the front lines were overfull. The city of Iassy could not take any more wounded, and it has been decided to transfer the lighter cases in smaller cities, Vaslui being the nearest.

Red Cross organized special training courses for the young who wanted to work in the hospital. There were plenty of volunteers who enrolled in training, and from the first day they have been in contact with the problems of the hospital with the assistants, and the doctors. Teodora, being prepared by Iulia, was already familiar with most of the medical problems and examinations. After two months of training and after the final exam, Iulia's assistant took the diploma with congratulations.

Teodora was over joyful. It was something that surpassed her expectations. Retrospectively she remembered how much she wanted to go to school in Vaslui as her older brothers, but her parents preferred to keep her beside them at home. Alexandru was officer and Iorgu was a teacher with a rank of sub-officer. The boys have been taken to war. After two month of their enrollment, they have been listed disappeared. Who knows in what explosion or bombardments their bodies have been pulverized or covered by mud or dust. The parents remained in eternal waiting, hoping, wandering that they are around somewhere, and perhaps they will return home.

Catrina always keep praying at the church, but was going to the witch also who encouraged her, telling her that the sons are healthy and will be coming home very soon and the poor mother was waiting for them.

When Teodora married, although she didn't remain with them in the village, they were relieved that their daughter became the wife of a ranger. Maybe, in secret, they regretted that haven't sent her to school.

But God turns things as He things, and now Teodora was medical nurse, just as she desired. Her satisfaction was shadowed by the thought that she couldn't enjoy this realization together with Dragomir, who she felt always near her.

In the hospital, the young nurse received only praises and recognitions which were warming her soul. Teodora asked all wounded soldiers if they saw Dragomir. Unfortunately, no one had seen him.

The town hall of Pungeşti was receiving news from the frontline. Some men were listed as disappeared, others have been taken prisoners. The dead people were notified through a paper edged with black. The families who received letters were looking first at border, and then read the content. If the border was not black they were hopeful.

Teodora was pregnant in the eight month, and Iulia helped her to choose the cloth that would hide her pregnancy, and so, her pregnancy went unnoticeable. It appeared to be a plump woman. Her health and energy didn't diminish, though she was crying every night.

Iulia advised her not to go to the hospital, in order to avoid stressful situations.

Many wounded left home disfigured without hands, without feet, with scars on their faces and bodies, but happy and thankful to be alive. Teodora would have wanted Dragomir back in any situation. Her heart was going to pieces when Mihai was calling daddy. Because Ana and Mihai had two mothers Iulia and Teodora, but only one daddy, Manea. They have been raised from the beginning in a total harmony, being too small, in order to receive an explanation.

Although the family Manea had a good housekeeper, the children were all day long together under the supervision of Vasilica in Teodora's garden, where it was quite. But on weekends and holidays all got together and had lunch at Manea's family.

It was Sunday; the table was ready for lunch, when doctor Manea came home enraged. Iulia and Teodora noticed that something went terrible bad. Teodora started immediately to cry thinking that there could be a bad news about Dragomir. The Doctor quietly told them that it's not about Dragomir but about their friends from Pungeşti who fled to Câmpulung at Berta's relatives. The Jews from Câmpulung have been deported with a train of death in Transnistria. Isidor died in the train and Berta is alive. In the summer they'll manage but in the winter almost all will die because winters in Transnistria are dreadful and refugees don't have clothing, food or medicine.

Teodora took her maternity leave and was constantly busy preparing the room for the baby on his way. Cloth and nappies had enough left from Mihai. She bought another crib because Mihai was still using his; he needed a bed with bars. He was full of energy and a boisterous little boy without this bed he would be found every morning on the floor.

On Sunday she was going to the church with St. Paraschiva's relics, out of the Traian's square where she lit candles for the dead but also for the health of the living. After the church service she returned home in a better mood, quiet and at peace.

On a morning at the end of August she felt that she is ready, the baby was coming. Vasilica accompanied her to the doctors Iulia and Teodor Manea. Iulia consulted her and immediately prepared the room for birth. Vasilica has been sent home to take care of the children. The birth pains started and so did the contractions which became more frequent, sign that the birth will be easy, without hassle. Within a few hours in the world arrived a little healthy boy, a little darker skin, sign that was Dragomir's child. From the list of names Teodora picked Gabriel. She wanted that both boys would celebrate their name day together, at the saints Archangel Mihail and Gavril.

It would have been normal to inform Dragomir but no one knew where he is located. The front, after information received, was at Stalingrad

*

In Pungeşti, at town hall, were arriving daily notices about soldiers being taken prisoners in Stalingrad or at the Don's Elbow.

On the eve of the winter holidays the grandfather Gherasim made a visit to his grandchildren, loaded with all sorts of traditional gifts. Actually, the main purpose was another one, but he didn't know how to deliver the good news, but not too good. Teodora sensed that his father-in-law is not in his waters, and asked him directly what has happened. At the town hall of Pungeşti arrived a notice that the sergeant Dragomir Simionescu has been taken prisoner at Don's Elbow. Teodora masking the pain exclaimed with a faked joy: "Oh, Lord, good thing that he's well and he is alive, I'm sure he will be back healthy! Father, let us not lose hope!"

They continued the conversation and the grandfather took the little one in his arms. He was Dragomir's mirror and regained his optimism.

He departed for canton on the same day, because the holidays were approaching and many people were coming to "buy" firewood without money.

The English and Americans began bombing. The first bombs have fallen over Ploieşti. The Germans refurbished the petrol campus with new modern equipment to become more profitable for them.

The following air raid had the main objective the capital Bucharest. Simultaneously they bombarded other capital cities from Europe: Rome, Berlin, Sofia.

The residents from the capital city incurred tens of alarms, and only a few were false in the sense that the airplanes have had as target other cities. Those who had relatives or friends in villages around Bucharest took temporarily refuge in the suburbs, were most times had to pay rents.

The birds of steel appeared without program, at any time: morning, afternoon, evening or at night. Missiles "grapes lights" changed the night in day the bombs were dropped with a mathematical precision. Many cities have been destroyed by the bombing: Turnu Severin, Iassy, Roman, Târgu Frumos, Vaslui and many others.

The people from Vaslui didn't expect that their small city without strategic objectives to be bombarded.

Because the front was approaching fast the Prut River, all cities in the vicinity were full of Germans who were waiting to be sent to front.

The German commandment in Vaslui was located on the Tudor Vladimirescu Street, in the house of Haimovich, one of the richest merchants of the city. In 1941 all his family left the country.

The Germans took the house as it was. They moved the furniture from a room to another, throwing away what was unnecessary. They hanged their swastika flag; they installed powerful lighting, and permanent guard, that nobody dared to circulate on the street without fear. The locals were careful not to interfere with the sentinels. If any child dared to play the ball away from their home's gate, the sentinels, pointed their arms at the poor child who, frightened, ran away, as fast as he could.

When the bombardment started, the commandment took serious measures of camouflage at night, and when they were informed that the bombers have begun. The entire street entered in a total darkness.

*

March 1944. A rumbling like in the great earthquake of 1940 shook the city of Vaslui from its foundations. On the blue sky the huge birds showed up with an incredible noise. The heavy bombardiers flew slowly as even didn't move at all. The hunting planes flew low and fast as the lightening.

Above the city, in the past, similar big planes passed but higher in the sky, designated for other destinations.

People realized the danger only after the first bombs fell on a wing of the building where the German commandment was. Bombs have fallen into multiple rows that the whole building has been made one with the ground. The entire street has been destroyed, and only one house remained standing. It was the house of Costache, servant of the church and God has placed his hand over it.

The building that provided the anti-air sounds was the first to be hit. By the time when they regrouped the planes were far away above Roman.

A few hunting aircrafts have concluded the attack in which the Tudor Vladimirescu street was completely destroyed, and not this one but also other streets, at random.

Until then the bombardments were done only in large cities and people in Vaslui didn't know how to react in these moments. They didn't know that they need to hide underground or protective places.

Iulia and Teodora were returning from the hospital toward the house, loaded with small bouquets of snowdrops and other spring flowers. They bought them from an old woman at the corner street. They bought all the flowers from the old woman, giving her also extra money, so she didn't have to stay longer on the street. To their generosity the old woman replied with "Let God give you health, mother!" and left slowly on the road towards Redin.

The young ladies, observed that the airplanes come lower than normal, and panicked, not knowing which way to go. To go to the hospital, which under international law was protected, (although there were cases, when by mistake, during the night rides some hospitals have been bombarded), or to run fast toward the house to the children.

In a second though, the first bomb fell down. Trembling with fear, holding their hands, they laid down on the ground as other people.

The majority of people, especially children, were screaming, and running confused on the streets. Only now the residents of Vaslui understood what it means war.

The dead people from the combats of Vaslui and The High Bridge, during Ştefan the Great, were calling with mute voices the followers to keep them company.

The streets Petru Rareş, Ştefan The Great, Tudor Vladimirescu and others have been crushed by bombs, each square meter. The German Central commandment was burning in the flame of Hell. An artificial thick fog and a choking smoke covered the city. The bells of the churches covered the cries of help. The old bell of the old church "Saint Ioan the Baptizer" built by Ştefan the Great, in the year 1490, sent out sad vibrations from the old times.

Teodora, covered by the clutter of the crumpled building that fell near was holding Iulia's hand that could not be seen. She wanted to get up but her feet were kept back by a mountain of bricks that covered all her body. Any call for aid was in vain because nobody heard and yet did not see anything. Any call for help was inutile; no one could hear, or see anything. A tap of the body opened and she felt how her blood was running through.

In this confusion, in a state of lethargy and exhaustion, she felt that she is going to faint. She was squeezing Iulia's hand, but she didn't answer. Through her mind were flying all sorts of images as in a dream, and all were in connection with their children. She remembered the two boys who died, when they passed the threshold of six months. That Mihai still lives wearing two souls. He will be, probably, a big man. Then she had a brightening illusion; she'd like to cross herself but she couldn't, maybe with the tongue but she could not.

She saw a huge skeleton of burned bones looking as the statue of death, with the eyes big black holes, and a big scythe of fire that reached the sky. All of a sudden the skeleton broken into pieces taking fire from the scythe. In an instant from the immense figure didn't remain anything, not even the ash. The image changed into a garden with spring flowers and snowdrops. No, it cannot be the Heaven's garden. Stepping over the flowers was playing three children: they are Ana, Mihai and Gabriel. Mihai was three and half years. He was quiet and well behaved. Ana, the little girl found in the basket was of the same age. Perhaps she was younger or older than Mihai. Manea family before adopting the little girl made a discrete research in the birth certificates archives of Jews children from Iassy, but wasn't able to establish who were Ana's parents. The idea to write in the new certificate as date of birth the same birth date as Mihai's has been accepted by all. Gabriel not yet two years old but he was trying to keep up with the other two siblings. Sometimes he stood on his small chair, and with his little hands was directing the other two. "This one will be general, Heaven forbid", joked the doctor.

The sirens of the ambulances announced that the bombardment is over for now, leaving behind a disastrous scene. Doctors, health assistants collected the wounded and the dead. Of course they had to give priority to the German machines, but nearly all ranking Germans were dead. German boots and heats were found were found riddled, discarded for hundreds of meters or almost burned.

Teodora was noticed by a medical crew being covered almost entirely with plaster and bricks. She was holding tight Iulia's hand. The ruins have been removed with care but the woman still felt its weight. She opened her eyes screamed in despair, Iulia, Iulia!

After a couple of minutes, they got rid of all the debris, the scene transformed in a nightmare, which cannot ever be forgotten. In the place next to her, covered by bricks was no longer Iulia but only her hand. Teodora felt stunned by the sight was tightly holding Iulia's hand to her chest, as a child and lost her conscious.

She woke up in the hospital, repeating continuously delirious: "Give me the child, Iulia, Iulia". Next to her was Dr. Manea totally worried out. They gave her heavy sedatives and she fell asleep guarded by a nurse.

The wounds seemed superficial but it was imposed a careful supervision for a couple of hours or even days. The fall of the wall could produce internal injuries that could not be noticed immediately.

At the head there were no visible hematomas, and no open wounds, probably she had suffered only a great shock. As far as Iulia, her death occurred suddenly hit by shrapnel flying across that decapitated her, cutting off her arm. The remaining of her body was carefully gathered and was placed in a closed coffin.

Ana was left for the second time without mother, but she knew nothing and may she will never know the truth. "Lord, where have you been? Maybe you fall asleep up there for just when the death's scythe reaped Iulia, the most kind and generous human being."

Dr. Manea, the most affected of them all, had managed by a supreme effort, to hide the pain, the revolt and bitterness inside his soul. The tears were also internally.

Teodora, couldn't be convinced not to participate at her friend funeral, she was brought in a wheel chair from some German facilities.

The children did not understand too well the phenomenon of death but were crying when they were told that Iulia left up in the sky from where she'll look after them always.

They have been taken home, before they lower the coffin in grave. Such a scene would have been hard to bear.

The priest Andrei, who was give some medicine to calm him down, was reacted by saying only: "Hallelujah" and "God bless". He was living the tragedy of his life. He suffered when his wife died, but now, his brain was exploding of pain. His soul was hanging dangling between belief and not belief. Victorious, however, was his faith forgiving God. Perhaps, up there in Heaven was needed a good doctor as Iulia.

After the funeral, Teodora didn't want to go back to the hospital for nothing in the world. She promised to the doctor that she'll sit quietly in bed, only to be with the children who knew that their mother is ill and must not go, as Iulia did.

Vasilica supervised the children engaging them in quiet plays, never the less a hidden sadness was nesting in their fragile souls. With a mature understanding they approached the mother's bed caressing her hands, her hair, and her face. "Did the pain pass?" was asking Ana with mature care. "Yes", answered Teodora, swallowing her tears. She felt that she's at the end of her powers and she could not understand where from were still coming all these tears of sorrow. Her heart collected a surplus of suffering and it was ready to explode. The children's death, the rebellion, the war, Dragomir's disappearance and Iulia's death, all of these was too much for her.

*

The war tipped its balance in the favor of Russians who crossed the Prut River. The Germans didn't have any chance; everywhere they were hunted and killed.

In the meantime in the territory of the Soviet empire, had been formed the division of volunteers "Tudor Vladimirescu" composed of Romanian prisoners, who have decided to fight alongside the Russian troops, until the final victory.

The division, armed, entered into struggle against the Germans near Vaslui, at Bulboaca and Deleni. Among volunteers was also Dragomir, who would have preferred to be injured, but the bullets were going around him.

A man from the vicinity of Pungești taking advantage of ambush that took place proposed to Dragomir to run together. Dragomir wasn't a coward, and advised Costică not to defect.

A few defector soldiers, who by chance have passed through their village, trying to run away, have been shot on the spot without being considered for court-martialed.

Costică has never been seen anywhere. Maybe he run away or perhaps had been injured and he was in the hospital.

Dragomir, with luck, found a scrap of paper on which he wrote a few words and put it in the pocket of an injured solder that was transported to the hospital in Vaslui.

Following the battles near Vaslui, the hospital was full of Romanian and Russian wounded.

At the hospital's gates the German's place was taken by the Russian soldiers.

The medicines, syringes and other medical instruments remained from Germans found now an immediate use.

An injured Russian soldier was wearing around his hand five watches "war capture", lined up one near the other almost to the elbow. But there was no room for comments.

Hospitals' staff met now for the first time women officers of high rank and had a special respect for the women officers. The Russian women were beautiful, midwives, brave, reliable, gentle and civilized. Two of them, perhaps, medical staff, followed attentively the medical staff at surgeries and post recovery recuperation of the wounded.

Teodora, through gestures, was able to communicate to one of them that her husband is on the front and has three children at home. The Russian woman smiled with affection and the next day brought her candies and Russian chocolate for the children.

The injured man, who had the note from Dragomir, had the opportunity to give it, by chance, to Dr. Manea. The note was brief: "I am healthy. I miss all of you, especially Mihai and Teodora. We'll see you soon, Dragomir." The doctor, with much calm asked the wounded a couple of questions about Dragomir. The injured man didn't know Dragomir, he saw him only when he placed the note in his pocket. About the subject of war, battle or imprisonment was no reason to ask anything.

Teodora was no longer in the hospital so the doctor hurried to take the news as soon as possible to her. She kissed the note received; it was as a piece of sky. The joy was too great. She was skipping around like a child, repeating continuously: "Dragomir lives!" The children didn't understand anything, but they repeated after Teodora "Dragomir lives" participating at mother's joy. Their concepts about life, death, family ties, brother, sister were unclear.

Since Iulia's death, Ana lived in Teodora's house knowing that Mihai and Gabriel were her brothers. Vasilica was in charge of the children and she was very devoted. They were her soul.

That night, seemed for Teodora without end. She looked at the clock many times. Early in the morning, she was the first nurse from her shift that entered the hospital gate. The injured man with the note from Dragomir was operated. Dr. Manea accompanied her at the bed of the wounded, but could not find out anything more. After a couple of weeks of hospitalization, the injured man, called Vasile, remained with a serious handicap, and was discharged. He returned to his village in the Bacău County. Other wounded from the first division "Tudor Vladimirescu", who recovered have been sent again on the west front. Teodora sent messages for Dragomir with all departing solders announcing him, most of all, that he has a son.

The message received from Dragomir was too great not to be shared with his father and father-in-law. The next day, Doctor Manea sent a telegram note to the Mayor Tăbăcaru of Pungești, which he knew for many years, asking him to announce Gherasim Simionescu that he's expected in Vaslui to receive good news. Teodora, but especially children, would have wanted to go back to the forest as they did almost every Sunday, but now they could not go because of unsafe road.

Long columns without end of armored tanks, trucks, motorcycles, flowed ceaselessly from Iassy.

Sometimes rambling or intentionally taking side roads looking for food products. Not all the soldiers were friendly with the locals population, which, for fear, were hidden themselves in the corn fields or in the forests.

A walk up to canton was excluded. But the old Gherasim, who knew all the places as his own hand, could go through without difficulty, by walking or on horseback in the woods in the forest, from a village to another village, through hidden places.

In fact, even without the old telegraph the old man was prepared to leave the next day to Vaslui having the same news received from the runaway Costică.

The battles from Vaslui ended and the Russian army troops and those of the Division "Tudor Vladimirescu" destroyed another German church and were on their way to Bucharest.

At the canton, after the battles from Bulboaca, in the middle of the night, although gates were well locked, Gherasim heard some knocks at the window and then at the door.

He got his gun and asked "who is it?"

The Russians could not penetrate the forest depths up to the canton. The scared voice replied: "It's me, Costică, I ran away from the battlefield." The ranger opened the door cautiously, listening to know if there are other fugitives or not.

Costică enters the house like an arrow but in the middle of the room he collapsed on the floor, saying with difficulty two words "water" and "food". Gherasim brought him a cup with milk which the runaway drank it breathlessly, asking for another. From the fresh bread brought by the ranger he began to eat as a hungry wolf.

After he eats some, and his hunger wasn't as painful, he told how he was able to flee in the middle of the Bulboaca battles. He asked also Dragomir to be his companion, but that he refused. Gherasim asked him all sorts of questions in connection with his son. He had learned with joy that Dragomir lives. The next day would have to go to Vaslui to give the news to Teodora. Costică said many things about front and about imprisonment, terrible things, unbelievable, for one who didn't ever go to war.

Conditions of imprisonment were hard and not too far from the Nazi camps. The truth was that the Russian people warred out, became very poor. They could not afford to feed the prisoners who fought against them. The basic food made from potatoes peels, moldy cabbage, half boiled, was given to those prisoners who were working all day difficult and dangerous jobs.

Costică left from home three years ago and now he returned weak, toothless, as a hound, shivering of sickness and of fear, his voice husky and totally weak. The Ranger promised not to disclose anything, but he has to stay hidden until the end of war. If anyone else finds about him, they both will be taken before the court-martial: one deserter, and the other accomplice.

At the first light of the day Gherasim started to walk to Vaslui on roundabout ways, known only to him. At dusk he arrived at Teodora which with great joy showed the note that she received from Dragomir. In the house was real celebration. Harvested berries and raspberries collected during the night by Costică added more gaiety to the children who were singing in choir what they heard from their mother: "My father is alive, my father is alive" without knowing which father lives.

The news that she wanted to bring to Teodora was shadowed seeing the note from Dragomir. About Costică, the grandfather didn't say a word knowing the repercussions such secrecy would have if caught.

After they put the children to bed, Gherasim prepared to make immediately the road back to canton. The paths that he took were places well known and the horse knew them too well.

He found Costică as frightened as he was when he left, listening to any noise from the forest.

Even though the front had moved away, the earth was still shacking. When the tanks were silent the airplanes began as though there was a schedule. The hunting airplanes lagging behind the heavy bombardiers, were lining the sky like shuttles of fire.

The anti-air artillery from Vaslui was quiet for a few days, a clear sign that the east part of the country was under Russian occupation and the Germans, with all their faded glory, were returning to their homes simply ravenous of burden.

The Soviet Army, in offensive, without stopping, occupied Bucharest. Hitler's forces in a last effort and stubbornness bombed the city. Has been destroyed National Theater built a century ago, damaged many institutions such as: The Royal Palace, the University and Museum "Grigore Antipa".

Romania joined United Nations.

The war continued a while on the Romanian ground and produced tens of thousands of dead, wounded, and lost.

Vaslui County Hospital being too far away from the front line did not receive any more wounded. But at town halls, the mayors continued to receive news about the fate of the wounded soldiers, from the battlefield.

*

At the beginning of October, on a misty day, cold, without sun, the old ranger Gherasim came in a great hurry in the city, he stopped directly at the hospital. He searched for Dr. Manea, because the news he brought for Teodora could kill her. The nurse, invited by the doctor believed that there is a professional problem. Seeing her father-in-law, with his face whiter than usual, in her mind was running all kind of thoughts, all scary. At the Doctor's gesture the nurse sat, but she felt that the seat was full of a hedgehog spikes. Gherasim, strongly marked, could not articulate any word and only placed the note on the table, in front of his daughter-in-law. She read and became dumb with pain, as if a claw of an eagle mangled her body and soul. "Dragomir had fallen heroic in the battles for the liberation of Oradea city". Her clenched jaws couldn't allow her to open her mouth, and the glass with water provided by the doctor had turned into a jaw of a shark, ready to tear her apart. She regained some of her senses and the locked tears of the impact have spurted like cold spills, almost icy, streaming down her white and inert cheeks.

The range frightened, was making desperate gesture to the doctor who beckoning back tranquil was trying to comfort him. He offered to Teodora the cup of water asking her to drink just a little bit. She drank all the water because there was an internal thirst produced by an imaginary burning fire.

After a short pause, at the doctor's insistence, she got up on her feet, dizzy and disoriented. Walking as with foreign legs she left herself in the hands of the doctor and her father-in-law who took her home. At home, the doctor told to Vasilica and to the children that mother is ill and needs to be let alone in her room.

The children understood, and turned their attention to their grandfather Gherasim, circled him, and waiting for the usual goodies brought for them. The grandfather too affected by the death of his son, left in a hurry from the town hall and forgot about everything else. He didn't bring to the children any sweets as he used to do every time when visited his grandchildren. Quickly he pulled from his pocket a couple of coins and asked Vasilica to go and buy something for the children. Vasilica entered the hallway, when the doctor whispered something to her. The woman, shocked in terror, sketch a soft wail, covering her mouth with the hand. She returned quickly loaded with candies of all colors, and fondant brightly colored, these were the only sweets in the small shops, in time of war.

The grandfather remained overnight in Vaslui to the great joy of the children who had numberless of questions: "What color are the leaves of the trees, if the nuts have fallen yet, why he didn't bring any pears, which birds have left and when they'll be back." The Grandfather responded to them only by moving his lips because his thoughts were elsewhere, to the Dragomir's soul lost somewhere. The children went to bed with the promise that the grandfather will not go away until the next day. Dr. Manea told Teodora to take a sleeping pill, and then he left toward his house, rather affected.

The next day, Teodora woke up dizzy, because she never took a sleeping pill before. So much pain sprouted in her body and her heart as though an orchestra directed by a magic baton intone funeral music. Children were watching with sadness in her eyes waiting for a smile or even a sweet word. She hugged and kissed them taking one at a time tight to her chest, she felt that she was able to subdue her tears.

The children were too small to understand the problems and feelings of the old people, so, perhaps, it will be necessary that they be protect; she will tell them a children story.

Vasilica was preparing, as usual, the breakfast. In the house smelled of boiled milk. "Grandfather," said Ana, "why the milk comes up and then flows out of the pot?" "Because it doesn't like to be boiled and it wants to get out and run away", said grandpa. "Poor milk, let's not boil it" said Ana.

This dialog made Teodora to switch, for a moment, her thoughts to the children.

The grandfather left pursued by the grandchildren's sweet voices competing in their good wishes and requests for next visit.

Teodora couldn't go to the hospital; she felt the need to think at what will follow.

Gherasim went at his relative Nestor, on Traian Street, where he left his horse, at this time he was depressed and couldn't talk much; he jumped on the horse and left for canton.

He buried two wives, had suffered a lot, but the unexpected death of his son went so far beyond any pain. As a fallen oak, with the trunk and its branches cut he felt helpless in the face of the implacable destiny. He had emerged out of time, aged, the energy left his body, and nothing could be as yesterday.

Teodora was moving in the house like a ghost, overwhelmed by dark images and thinking.   When her first child Dumitru died, she believed that her brains were burning. At Mihai's death, she didn't have time to realize the moment, when the Lord recovered His mistake giving her another Mihai to comfort her.   The loss of Iulia and now of Dragomir reopened all the wounds, which she believed were cured. The death travesty in an invisible phantom was following her, and she didn't know why? She needed time, peace, and the love of those around her. Dr. Manea stopped by their house on his return from the hospital. He was happy to hear the news that Teodora had planned to go with the children at the canton and then to Gârceni.

He confessed that he wanted to suggest to her to do this, but he did not know what Teodora plans and reaction would be. Of course, that all were due to leave with the doctor's car next day, after the doctor will end his visit at the hospital.

The road to Pungeşti was open and good, although the weather didn't cooperate being quite grim.

The first stop was made at the Jewish cemetery of Pungeşti. The children remained in the car with Vasilica. Teodora and Manea went directly to the Isidor's family grave where Mihai was buried. They didn't shed tears, keeping only a moment of mourning in the memory of those who were sleeping peacefully under the crypt of stone. With the recollection in their souls they continued the road to the canton.

In the car, the children were wondering, quietly, why there is no more joy as it used to be other times, their mother did not sing and the father was sad and tense.

At the canton, the children regained their joy, bless by the red sun of autumn. They stopped directly at fowler's pear searching at the bottom, among rusty leaves, the sweet-sour fruits which were a little astringent on their mouth and lips. In the yard the grandfather was working helped by a skinny man, who spotting the people at the gate ran with quick steps, to the enclosures behind the house.

"Who's that man?" asked curiously Ana.

"A man alone, as me, I took him in to keep me company this winter", said the old ranger, hiding the truth about Costică.

While the kids were playing as in the good days, the parents retracted in the house and were discussing things related to the death of Dragomir. The old Gherasim, a convinced faithful, said that it would be desirable to make for his son a traditional funeral. Only that in the coffin, when the dead, for various reasons, didn't exist, will be placed a suite worn by the deceased.

Teodora was still hoping that her husband is not dead. Perhaps those who sent the notification were wrong and Dragomir is injured or he lost his memory, who knows where he is wandering and one day he'll return home.

Her father-in-law was trying to persuade the woman that the notices of the lost loved ones were specifying the place and the conditions in which the facts occurred. Teodor wished that at the end of the war she'll personally go to the common grave where he was buried and, together with other families who lost their loved ones, would build a monument in the memory of the heroes who died on the battle field.

Dr. Manea assisted neutral, to the discussion, and realized that Teodora's too distress to be contradicted on her thoughts.

He begged Gherasim to postpone the controversy, at least for some time, until Teodora will revise her thinking, which at this time is not coherent. The old man, sympathetically, changed the discussion, returning to children. The little ones with their rosy cheeks were talking with the wild doves, which were lined up on the fences as for a countdown.

By evening they left for Gârceni. Teodora's parents didn't know yet about the Dragomir's death. They enjoyed enormously seeing their grandchildren, which they didn't see since the Russians arrival. The doctor downloaded their luggage from the car and taking advantage of being alone with grandfather Rotaru told him, in short, about Dragomir's death. He cautioned him that his nephews don't know anything about it and it would be best if they do not know.

Shortly after the doctor kissed the children said good bye and left. He didn't want to get caught by the dark on the road.

Teodora entered in her room, which remained unchanged decorated only with the white chrysanthemums picked from the garden.

In the living room and kitchen there were a lot of baskets with fresh fruits, dispersing a paradisiacal fragrance.

The grandmother was already with her hands into the dough to make some pies "charm-n-strap", the delight of the children, who were having a heated argument in the yard with two turkeys brandishing their tail as a fan, and showing the red beads with fury. The little ones with sticks in hand, longer than them, were trying to undermine the authority of the chief supreme bosses of all the birds in the yard.

Several months later Teodora, with lucidity, understood that Dragomir couldn't come back, accepting the proposal from her father-in-law to organize a funeral ceremony with the participation of relatives and friends. The children, as during Iulia's funeral didn't participate.

At the end of the month October, 1944 the whole territory of Romania was liberated. But the war continued until the total defeat of Hitler.

*

The hunt against the Jews has been stopped only at the end of the war.

The Romanian Government issued a decree in regards to the statute of nationalities, which stipulated that "all citizens are equal before the law without reference to race, nationality, language or religion."

The Jews who survived returned to their homes, and most of them went to Israel. Wise and conciliators they do not bear against anyone, no bitterness on the understanding that the history also has its black spots.

Costică remained hidden fearful at the canton, until the end of the war. When the first solders began to return to their homes, he showed up also in the village, dressed in his tattered soldier's uniform, which, inspirationally, was kept hidden in the poultry cottage at the canton. The soldiers came from different companies or different units, so on the battle lines was little chance that two people from the same village will met. Each of them was talking about their committed braveries on the font, describing bits of retained images. One said that passed over the bridge with lions in Budapest; another one that he had seen in Prague, in the tower city, a large cuckoo clock and its various figures. Only Costică was not bragging about anything, but he played well the role of ignorant. Slowly, slowly, collecting from here and there what others said, made for him a story to which he added colorful scuttlebutt, and he was telling it with all that excitement, that made it believable. And the runaway, who became a hero, was the first to enroll in the new party which was the only one in power over the whole country for nearly half a century. He built a house, got married and entered in politics as the most honest communist. Due to its merits on the battlefield, about which he always mentioned, he even became the party secretary. The old pensioner Gherasim, retired in his house in the village, was marveling at Costică's courage. But he had character, and kept the secrecy lucked with seven padlocks. One day, he found out that the secretary of the party was after the land of the ranger Ioan Simionescu, labeling him as public reactionary, and made a trip to city hall where was also the location of the party organization.

"I'm looking for the comrade party secretary", said Gherasim very loud to be heard by all. Costică came out of his office and mumbling something invited the pensioner inside to sit down. The former ranger who provided to the deserter with sanctuary in his canton without telling anyone a word began the discussion:

"Costică, my son is not reactionary, neither agricultural peasant to enter into collectivization, he is a public civil servant, he is serving the country, and he has to be respected as such. The land is his wife's and only she can decide if she wants to switch to collectivization or not."

Costică understood immediately what was all about, he invoked at first big words read in the newspapers, then embarrassed, subsided. In conclusion he ensured the old man that no one in the county will consider the brigadier an "enemy of the people".

But the ranger was with his head above others, so he took all the necessary measures to position his family such that it doesn't have to suffer. He was a great lover of books and could not accept that his sons would not be able to benefit from high education.

Three of the children have been fictional adopted by some poor relatives; a part of the land has been given to some people without any land, and so he remained with four hectares, dropping below the line that would have labeled him as wealthy (kulak).

Costică could have researched the whole situation but he had to keep silent, his own situation was such that his hands and feet were tied. He remained silent even after the death of the old Gherasim being sure that his secret is now hidden forever.

The brigadier's children attended the highest schools, becoming valuable people even in the poor conditions in which they lived. For the children of poor people and for those of party organizers the gates of all schools have been wide open. From them entered the school who wanted, emerging learned only those who were capable.

*

The time had lost its patience; it was flying by with gigantic steps over another time, past, leaving deep marks and being the witness of the present, and the future. The war ended but its shadow was feeding from the open wounds preventing their healing.

Dr. Manea, who went himself through the Caudine Forks of fate, hoped that once the war ended he'll take his life from the beginning, especially for children's future with whom he was totally connected. Life's experience, the lucidity and his moral condition were the pillars of resistance on which he counted to a new life.

The interminable discussions with Teodora had also a hidden purpose: to test the feelings and the future intentions for the young woman. He had tried a few times to suggest the idea of joint future, but each time the discussion broke in the same place, blocked.

"Teodora", he concluded the discussion, "nothing in life is easy, even life itself."

Children were growing up nicely because their tiny souls were not touched by the killer dust of the hurricane produced by the war and its consequences.

Ana and Mihai were blond and you could swear that they were born of the same mother. Teodora was very happy when people were saying that both children look like her. It was a perfect coincidence, because the truth remained behind, swallowed by time and may never resurface.

Gabriel was the perfect image of his father Dragomir. He had a volcanic character trying with tenacity to be as good as his older siblings, and to surpass them sometimes.

"When I'll be big and you'll be small, you'll do only what I'll tell you." Ana and Mihai were surprised by the lack of logic of their brother thinking, but they didn't contradict him, fact that would upset him.

Dr. Manea was, however, worried that although the three children knew each other as brothers and sister, when they'll go to school they'll find out that they have different last names.

There would require explanations not only to the children, but also to the authorities, perhaps with harsh consequences, which could affect the spiritual evolution of the children. The war, again the war, with its trailer pulled out of hell, passed over people, leaving behind ruins and cadavers wasn't forgotten yet. Not all ugly remembrances can be erased with a sponge, but some may be covered with silk curtains creating optical illusions. In time, some will be forgotten and will be replaced by other fresh memories, beautiful ones which will be easily accepted.

One day the doctor decided to tell Teodora everything that was on his mind about respect, friendship and admiration, love, duty for children and respect to all around him.

It wasn't the right time for declarations of love or romance scenes. If Teodora will judge rather with her mind, and less with her heart, there will be an option for a common future. The doctor kissed her hand with care and tenderness.

Teodora wasn't too much surprised by the doctor's proposal; perhaps she was thinking the same way.

She hugged the doctor with more tenderness as in the past. It was a positive response. The law of reason had won over the law of lost love.

It followed a few weeks of discussions between Teodora's family at which the children did not attend.

Catrina and Gică Rotaru were delighted by the decision of the two. Her father-in-law, the old man Gherasim, who withdrew to his house in the village, because the canton had a new younger ranger, did not oppose to the marriage. It was in the interest of his grandchildren's future, blood from Dragomir's blood, which left too quickly this life.

Father Andrei enjoyed the news with all his heart, kissing both of them and told Teodora that he'll adopt her as daughter. The priest was all alone, without close relatives, and the doctor's family was his family, and the children, all of them, were his grandchildren. The burden of old age for a man alone is sometimes heavy.

The marriage of Teodora and Teodor Manea was prepared in secret, and not even Vasilica knew.

Teodora became Mrs. Manea, but the children?

She could not accept, in her mind that the little Gabriel would not bear the Gherasim name. But Dr. Manea thought otherwise: All three children knew that they are brothers. When they'll go to school will be questions that may lead to misunderstandings. "Why, he will ask unaware, the twins have the name Manea and he Simionescu?" And then would be endless explanations which may, or may not be confusing and could have undesirable trauma for children.

The ranger Ioan Simionescu convinced his sister-in-law to the fact that the three children should not be separated.

The name, he argued, is a matter of formality, and sometimes a conjunction, especially in such tragic conditions through which they lived during the war.

The new birth certificates of the children became Manea's responsibility. It was not a thing too hard, but not easy either. Many people, after the war, were asking for new documents, because the old ones perished, burned, or were stolen; even some archives have been bombarded or devastated, the originals were missing, and the new certificates were made on trust or with witnesses. Dr. Manea had his man at city hall, Mr. Luca. The two of them knew each other for long and they knew many secrets which remained hidden.

Without anyone knowing, in a week, the doctor brought home new birth certificates for children: Ana and Mihai Manea were twins and Gabriel Manea was the little brother.

Teodora went to the St. John the New church, lit candles and kneeling in front of the icon of Saint Mary she prayed silently. "Forgive me Lord, forgive me Dragomir, I didn't keep your name, but I have done everything for our children's future. Only you, Virgin Maria, you can understand and forgive me".

When she left the church she felt that the heavy weight lifted from her soul and shoulders, and so, she firmly, made her first step on a new road.

Few months later she found out that she's pregnant. Teodora broke out in tears, which were mixed: salty, bitter-sweet of pain, hope, happiness, with an indescribable taste. Feelings unexpressed, emotions killed, unsatisfied thoughts, all of them, came out now through a flood of tears. Through them, she felt how the last drops of love for Dragomir were painfully drying out on a wire of fire that was still burning her.

She dried her tears, shaking all the dusty pain of her soul and walked alone on the streets. She wanted to make a confession but not to the priest, eventually to a human being from the street.

She was talking in her mind about her new happiness: Illusion or reality!

The child in her womb was Manea's; the small embryo was a mysterious gift which changed totally her vision of life. Other plans, other thoughts, other wishes resulted as the stars in the sky: at the beginning pale and then little by little finally becoming dominant and all-encompassing.

The news flabbergasted Manea, there were new feelings. The news swept over him with a new, unknown yet feeling to him. It became really hidden male and his dream will come true. Ana will retain its place: The little girl's too wise and beautiful.

For the newly wife and husband followed days and nights full of tenderness, and love. Years ago Manea craved after children. Soon their house will be full. He'll become father and his dream will come true. Ana will still remain his beautiful girl.

For the new pair followed days and nights full of tenderness, and love. Years ago Manea craved after children. Soon their house will be full of children. This was a heavenly blessing!

They imagined what kind of disputes will start between children when they'll find out that a new baby is on the road. Precisely, Ana will want a little sister and Gabriel, the rascal, will not accept with ease to trade its place of junior. But the news was enjoyed by all of them. The house was large enough, but some changes had to be made. Ana's room will remain the same. The little girl's mind was sharp and first objective was order and a sense of beauty. Although she was only five years, in her room there was nothing to spare and all the things were in order. The same was Mihai's room, Gabriel wouldn't ever clean his room, but because of the sibling's pressure, he felt somewhat ashamed and arranged his toys in his preferred order. Vasilica was doing daily over all cleaning, and they were helping her.

With everyone's agreement there have been made some changes. Gabriel's room was getting ready for the new baby. Mihai and Gabriel will live together sharing Mihai's room. Gabriel was glad that they'll be together and he will not be alone.

He wanted to sleep in the same bed with Mihai, but his parents cut it short, even before he expressed this wish, buying new furniture with two beds. Gabriel thought that's good enough. The relations between the two brothers have been sweetened. In the family was a total peace and quiet.

The declarations of love, uttered by Manea didn't were unprecedented. Each morning they awoke more serene, better and wiser.

*

The "free" elections from 1946 have been a sham that ended with mass arrests, threats and beats.   Following the so called elections, the historical parties, The National Peasant Party headed by Iuliu Maniu and the National Liberal Party of Ion Brătianu were eliminated by violence on the whole country, and dissolved.   The leaders of these parties as well as the representative members, some scholars, have been condemned without judgment and sent to prison.

The Deputy of the National Liberal party of Vaslui was Gheorghe Vrănceanu, world-renowned mathematician, born in the Hogii Valley.   The future academician, made his high school studies at the "Mihail Kogălniceanu" Lyceum from Vaslui.   He was the most noticed personality in the county.   Young, at the age of 46, he was gifted with a physical presence to be envied.   Rich black hair, high forehead; he seemed carved with an invisible chisel.   He used the warm Moldovian accent in all his speeches, and never forgot it all his life.   He was so well known that he didn't need any electoral propaganda.   He arrived at Vaslui only in the eve of the election, when he took a room at the Central Hotel.   He didn't inform anyone about his arrival.   He made only a phone call to Dr. Manea with whom he established to see each other after elections.   Dr. Manea, reserved, and cautions, didn't want to enroll in any party, although he had been asked. Perhaps he had his own reasons.

In the evening, after having dinner at the restaurant, the professor, in his pajamas, was sitting at a desk in his room, writing something, trying probably to resolve a problem.

Someone knocked persistently in the door. He, by nature, wasn't scared, and opened the door without asking who he is. He was shocked, to see in front of him a man big as a monster, dressed in a Russian uniform.   The Professor spoke French, English, Italian and German. He didn't know a word of Russian. But the strange visitor made it easy for him when him when he opened his mouth, speaking Moldovian. He could not understand why he was wearing Russian cloth, probably for intimidation. The intruder, very politely, begged him to take the first available train to Bucharest. He didn't provide any explanation, leaving on the table a train ticket for a sleeping wagon.   Instead of goodbye or apologize, the stranger insisted: "Please, don't miss the train, it's for your own good".

The mathematician, with his logic and intuition realized immediately that he is in big danger, and elections will be a scam. Disappointed, he went to the station, as the man suggested. At home there he found another proposal in connection with his candidacy to the National Liberal party. His wife found in the mail box an envelope with the following content: "We beg you to leave for a while the city of Bucharest. The signature was: A benevolent". The Professor didn't want any other inopportune visit as that from Vaslui. He decided to leave the capital the next day to Herculane, where he had a trusty friend, who was one of his students, and who hosted him with great pleasure. He had learned from press releases and on the radio that groups of hoodlums, some of them students, were going through schools and universities to intimidate the members of the historical parties.

Ioan Simionescu, a relative of the professor, enrolled in the same liberal party had a harsher treatment. When he got back home from voting, through the forest of Pungeşti, masked people beat him up with their fists and feet, "to teach him a lesson". Later he found out who those who attacked him, but he forgave them.

Following elections have been conducted in silence, only formally, because there was just one single party.

It is a saying that the evil is not coming alone and there a seed of truth in that.

A terrible drought which lasted two years covered Moldavia and Walachia regions. The rivers remained without water, from the fountains people were pulling out only mud. The rivers were dry and one could see only dry skeletons of fish and frogs. People started to sell their land, cattle and all the things from the house for a sack of corn meal. The clouds were like glued up on the sky and could not be pulled away.

Only the forests remained green because the trees, worthy creations of the nature, sucked grudgingly the water from the depths of the sick ground.

Above all these disasters came also the time when Romania needed to pay the debts of the war. Payments for the damages caused to Soviet Union amounted to huge sums have been converted to petroleum and natural gas, cereals, wood from the forests and many other products which had to be sent to the Soviet Union. The Moldovian which were closer to the border with the Soviet Union have been devastated without mercy. The trees cut and sorted by type and dimensions were sent in special freight trains to Soviet Russia. There have been some forests which have been speared under various pretexts. The plots have been marked as having trees too old, thunderstruck or infested with some red fungus. In most of the empty places they planted young trees which would take a quarter of a century to reach maturity.

*

The war left behind a shattered world, memories of nightmare, pain and suffering. At every step, you could see women and men dressed in black cloth, crippled youths. The dark shadows of the spillages of blood were still irritating the eyes and the human conscience.

The first snow covered only at the surface the misery left after the cruel massacre. Europe was under an improvised peace. The prisoners of war, only skin and bones, started to come back to their homes and life in small incremental steps and cautious crawling forward.

Through our villages, with an explained delay, from time to time were arriving forgotten prisoners from the cold Siberia. These were those who listened to their commanders, and didn't enroll in the divisions of volunteers. They were moving among people like some old robots as though someone washed their brains. They stayed away from people they didn't know, they didn't talk much, and above all they didn't divulge the living and work conditions in which they had been kept. The fear of not be sent again in the land of the ice bucket left them speechless and without hearing. The phantom of communism was still following them through our villages.

Those who returned, with the fear in their bones, did not hurry to become overnight communists. They stayed quietly, living without the red book of the party.

Not all who returned were lucky, after so many years away, to find their families. For some, their wives are re-married, many children were born, and the parents, aged and impoverished of sadness died. For all shortcomings and evils, the culprit has been the war.

In the summer of 1947, when no one expected the prisoner Pricop Cârlig from Gârceni returned. Tired after all this way, he stopped, and remained there in the middle of the village not knowing which way to go. He couldn't recognize his house. He looked around, but none of the houses looked as his. His memories had become opaque and knew no one. But he, too, was an unknown. Weak skeleton-like itinerant white dusty, he walked like a goose with his shoulders moving from left to right. He seemed out of hell, where he was tortured to carry heavy stones. After he went around the village, he spouted a house that looked like his. He knocked with uncertainty at the gate, pushed it with difficulty, and entered the yard. An old dog an approached him timidly.

"Azor," said Pricop, "is that you?"

The dog didn't bark but showed his teeth, as in a smile. Just then emerging from the summer kitchen was Saveta with a child in her arms and with another holding on to her skirt. He was thinking that perhaps he was hallucinating; otherwise how his wife would have two children that young. Nevertheless she was his wife.

"And you, who are you looking for? She said. "I'm tired of beggars."

The man pulled out his dirty, discolored hat, unveiling a bold head without any of his dark and rich hair.

"Is me, Pricop" opened his mouth, waiting for the woman's reaction.

"God, it can't be!" she whispered with a voice choked with tears.

Finally, the woman recognized the man, her husband who went to war. It had been since then almost seven years and she didn't receive any word. She performed all traditional church related ceremonies for her dead husband. Pricop participated in all battles and on the battlefield at Don's Elbow he was taken prisoner by Russians. When the division of volunteers Tudor Vladimirescu formed his commander didn't want to enroll, and he followed his command. Many others did the same and all have been sent to Siberia to labor camps. There, without Sundays or any other holidays they worked day and night, losing the notion of time.

After the end of war they thought that they'll be released, but it wasn't so. Perhaps their work was counted as the debts of war. Not even the locals treated them humanly, especially those who lost relatives in the war. For them these prisoners were viewed as those who killed their loved ones. Maybe they were right.

Saveta waited for a while, then she thought that Pricop was dead either shot down, eaten by the hungry wolves in Siberia or by the vultures in Caucaz, she decided to start all over. She is married, without religious wedding with a man who got lost or fugitive from Bessarabia. Sergey is a good man with the past forgotten. Together they have refurbished their home and already have two children. Now, if Pricop returned, this is his business, and she didn't even think to start another life all over.

The dog was seated and looked from one to the other, with undecided eyes. It would have said something but God hadn't given him the gift of speech. A bit of mind it had though because he recognized the master faster than Saveta.

The woman became more and more distress about the misfortune that happened to Pricop, and she proposed to stay a few days with them in the summer kitchen. Serghei was a good man and he'll understand the situation. Pricop didn't blame anyone, but he did not know what to do and where to start from. He had no home, he was nobody on this earth, he had only a soul too large for his small and ill body.

When Sergey came home, listened affectionately to the story and agrees with the proposal of his wife.

Next day, Saveta arose with a huge headache but full of ideas, all in favor of Pricop. She told him that Vasilica, the daughter of Spiridon, the one with a short leg, as they said, is in Vaslui, as housekeeper for Teodora who is Rotaru's daughter, who is now a big Lady. Dragomir, the ranger who was Teodora's husband died on the battlefield and she didn't wait long and re-married with Dr. Manea. During the war she went to a school of nurses and now she is the right hand of the doctor. They have a lot of children, and come often in Gârceni. In everything that Saveta said was a shred of truth, exaggerating and some smell of gossip. In the end she suggested to Pricop to go to Vaslui, to them, maybe they'll find some work for him, even, even street sweeper. Saveta's ideas were not bad and the man wanted to try them.

The woman gave him some cloth from Serghei, a clean shirt without patches, some old shoes, which were still holding on the feet, a bag with some food and told him to take the way to Vaslui.

The man, not having any other choice, and nothing to lose, thanked her for the cloths.

He took Saveta's advice and in one hour of walking barefoot, to save the shoes, he reached Pungeşti. But not even in Pungeşti things weren't as before. He didn't know anything about the rebellion, deportation of the Jews, the runaway of Jak and many other things. The beautiful village looked sad and everyone was in a hurry and sad.

The shops vanished; the sidewalks and streets destroyed full of pot holes, made by the passing Russian tanks, all were giving a painful sensation.

He wanted to buy a loaf of bread but Jewish bakeries were closed, and large webs of spiders were in abundance on the doors locked. Town hall was in the same place, and its walls needed paint, the plaster cracked everywhere during the war. The mayor was a dark-haired younger man, which Pricop didn't know.

Finally he found Pruteanu, a merchant. The prisoner told him his entire life story, asking for accommodations for a night's sleep. The man, impressed by Pricop's troubles received him with pleasure, giving him shelter.

Pruteanu told him about the Jews who have been sent to Transnistria leaving their bones over there. After the war only two came back, the only survivors. One had a Romanian lover married her, the other one has found his house occupied. He went to the grave of his forebears, and then he left for good the country in which he was born. With his watery eyes, the Jew would have said: "Lord, for three thousand years we are the chosen people, but now, I beg you, choose another".

Next day, from Pruteanu went to the drugstore, the same pharmacist, Mr. Lucian, who didn't know him, but listened with interest and compassion to Pricop's story, giving him at departure one hundred lei. "Lord, what a good man" was thinking Pricop, and was ready to kiss his hand in respect.

The journey to Vaslui was long and he traveled from wagon to wagon, being taken by various people. One going to Armășoaia brought him there, and then another one took him to Ivănești, and furthermore to Vaslui. To all he told his story. When he was stepping down the wagon each of them wished him "good luck and gave him whatever they could".

By evening he got to the hospital where the Manea family was working. He was looking for a lady named Teodora. A nurse, thinking that he is an ill patient, left quickly after Teodora, but before she left told him that in actuality Mrs. Teodora is Mrs. Dr. Manea. This was the name she was known, despite her disapproval. Teodora arrived, rather quickly and asked what the problem is, being ready to take place him in the consultation room. To his great pain Teodora did not recognized him either. He told her who he is and a short recount about his last seven years. Teodora looked astounded at the stranger who didn't look at all to the person she knew from their childhood.. He expressed his desire to be helped with a place of employment, anywhere, even street sweeper, as Saveta suggested.

"I've heard," he said, to be more convincing that Vasilica is your maid.

"No," replied annoyed Teodora, she is our person of confidence, keeps us house, taking care of children, because we are busy at the hospital."

Pricop lowered his head rather ashamed; it seems that Saveta didn't informed him well, and he kind of heat the water with a stich, and now was waiting now to clear it water. Teodora invited him to a cabinet, and asked him to seat on a chair. She left and Pricop remained to meditate: Teodora was the same as he knew her: with big blue eyes, with hair the color of the wheat ear, and a little more robust. But he wasn't able to call her by name, like in childhood, now she was a lady.

Within a short period of time she returned along with the doctor; already they had taken a decision: Pricop will live in Manea's house, in the room which was the birth hall, at the time when Julia was alive. Mrs. Teodora, put her scrub on the hanger on a hook, and dressed on her street cloth led the man home, leaving him in the care of Vasilica. She didn't recognize him, and this increased his sorrow. Vasilica looked better as when she was in the village. Dr. Manea studied her case and with some treatments and exercises, Vasilica no longer dragged her foot as before. Teodora encouraged her very much and she, now, was walking as well as everyone else in this world, they were ecstatic. Dressed nicely, with the hair combed with care in tail with a lovely colorful bow, Vasilica behaved like a well-trained housekeeper, and everyone in the house respected her.

The children, the twins, Ana and Mihai, were taken to school well-dressed in their ironed beautiful clothes. Everything was done by Vasilica; she took pride in taking care of all details.

Teodora told Pricop what he has to do: clean the courtyard and garden, take care of trees and flowers, and when necessary to help Vasilica with various chores around the house. The medical cabinet was next to the house and there was no garden. Between the two buildings there was a small gate for passing in the yard.

Teodora departed leaving Pricop in the care of Vasilica. The woman pointed at the room in which he'll reside asking him to clean it up. She brought him all sorts of clothes, shirts, boots all that the doctor didn't wear any more. She placed them in a cupboard, divided into two: categories: working clothes and clothes for the street. The things that Vasilica brought were so good that Pricop did not dare to put them on. She brought soap and showed him how and where to use the water for washing.

When the room and the corridors were ready Vasilica checked everything, declaring their readiness. She brought the bedding instructing him how to use all sorts of things, and then she invited him in the kitchen of the house, where she and the Manea family lived.

Poor Pricop no longer remembered how to eat with cutlery and never in his life did he see such silverware. For seven years he had eaten everything using his hand, like monkeys. He asked Vasilica to change his porcelain plate, being afraid it will break in his hands. Vasilica brought his food in a shallow dish of metal beautifully glazed and with all sorts of flowers all around the edges. After the meal she led him to his room, drawing to his attention to lock the doors and to turn off the light. Pricop slept as a log, a sleep that he didn't have since he was a child.

In the morning dressed in work clothes, as Vasilica ordered, went to his work .starting from the back yard, not to make noise, suspecting that all in the house are asleep. In the shade he found were all sorts of tools from which he has chosen those which he needed. It was early in the morning, and only few people were waling brisk on the street, maybe to the train station, he was thinking. The sun didn't risen yet and few clouds were wandered up in the sky, near the stars. The moon was in a hurry to pass the horizon before the rise of her beloved sun.

After about two hours, during which Pricop cleaned half of the garden, the doctor and his wife, left in a hurry, waiving at him good bye. And then the twins exited, led by Vasilica, only up to the gate. The school building was so close that when in session, you could hear the children's chirping in the garden.

Vasilica called Pricop for breakfast, asking him to firstly wash his hands. While he was eating came Gabriel. He sat down at the table next to Pricop and Vasilica insisted in vain to move into the living room. Moreover, he asked for a plate as nice as Pricop had.. Vasilica executed, immediately Gabriel's request, who became a little dictator. When Pricop went out to continue his work, Gabriel followed him, emulating everything Pricop was doing. "Take care of him" said Vasilica.

At lunch, the tweens returned home. They were well trained, and behaved under Vasilica supervision. The followed the same routine of washing hands, change cloth and prepare for lunch.

Ana exit through the back door calling for Gabriel. The boy followed the same ritual: washed hands, changed cloth and sat at the table. During lunch Gabriel boasted that he had eaten this morning in the kitchen, in a nice shallow dish in which you can beat with a fork without break it. To quiet him down, Ana told him that that is the cat's plate. Vasilica intervene quickly, to help Gabriel out and to defend his self-importance. "The cat's plate is at its place, and the plate in which Gabriel eat is a new plate metal glazed. I've just bought it from the market last month." All children had a good laugh.

When they came out to play and saw Pricop, they asked Vasilica who's the man. "A comrade who came from Russia", was the answer.

The children had a rigorous program and well thought, with hours of sleep, play and study. While the twins were doing their studies, Gabriel was put to draw; otherwise he would ask a zillion questions. He also played with a small German train toy received from the doctor as a gift. He also had many other toys, but his favorites were the solders. He had a nice collection of dozens of solders from all branches of the army: infantry, cavalry, hunter, mountain, border guards, tanks, etc.

After lunch, Vasilica sent Pricop in the city to get familiar where the market, drugstore, shops, etc. are. She handed him a sheet of paper on which she had written the street and number, in case he gets lost.

The man marveled as much this woman knows. He was thinking "Indeed, she is in charge with everything in this house!". She asked him to call her by name: You can call me Vasilica."

Pricop left as he was told. Wearing good, clean clothes he looked sharp, a gentleman. The only surprise was that not one in the city gave him any attention; everyone ignored him and all were walking in a hurry. He walked with increased attention so he'll remember what he sees and how to reach these places.

Before the war he went a couple of times in Vaslui, at various fairs, especially at the biggest of all at the beginning of September. From the pick of the hill where Nistor's house was you could see the fair very well. Now, it was only a fair of cattle and cereals. He climbed toward the center and found a large open market. At the market he found himself, he was at ease. Stroll into stands almost empty but did not find anyone he would know. Here and there were few peasants selling at high prices cheese, vegetables, fruits and even smoked beacon? He felt a great desire to taste a small slice of smoked beacon but did not dare to spend a dime from the money received from the pharmacist in the city of Pungeşti.

He got home without getting lost, changed into the working clothes and went to work. Until evening the garden was ready. The trees were cleaned of dead branches, and now they looked like girls with short hair and short skirts. The roses had been cut, about half a meter, as the gardening habits showed. All dead branches have been collected in small batches and prepared to be burned. However, he walked to the kitchen to ask Vasilica's permission. Vasilica was busy feeding Teodor. When the baby looked at the stranger he stretched out his hands toward him, trying to ask him who he is. Junior had been a year old and a few months. He knew many words but he couldn't put them in a sentence yet. "Comrade" she said. The child tried to repeat that word but came out something very strange as any other word that he heard for the first time. Pricop received Vasilica's approval to burn the branches. The fire was burning with large flames and the branches were moving as snakes, as they tried to escape from the fire. Pricop with a long fork was controlling the fire spilling the entire fiery pang guiding it toward finality. When the flames were quieted down, fading away, they had left behind two small swarms of ash that has been spread through the garden in place of other fertilizers.

At dinner, Ana who has retained from Vasilica the word comrade asked her father:

"Father, what does it mean comrade?"

The doctor gave her an explanation using simple terminology, and noticed that Ana was satisfied with it. The next day when she met Pricop her first question was:

"What are you doing comrade?"

Pricop was surprised by the question. He was fed up with the word comrade and he was afraid that he has come to a house or comrades. In time he became convinced that it's not so.

It had been a long two months since Pricop was working for the family and everyone was pleased with his service. In addition to clothes, food and home he received also some money. The food and quiet living showed on his appearance and he was beginning to look like Pricop people knew. The baldness, though, remained the same with only a few strips of white hair. With the head covered with the hat, he looked like Pricop from the past.

The doctor gave him some vitamins and medicines for his rheumatic pains. He eat and slept well and every morning he would wake up with a great desire to work. It seemed to him that the work was too easy for his energy. The Doctor took him each week to father Andrei where remained until the following day. The priest was very happy and praised him for his efforts. Several times he offered him money but Pricop refused. Pricop was telling him sometimes stories about his life in the Russian imprisonment. In Siberia, where he spent a couple of years he met other Romanians and Basarabians, who have been relocated by the Russians in those regions. One of his guards was from Basarabia. From that guard he heard some sort of a joke about communism and he told it to the priest. "In Moscow has been formed a train with the direction toward communism. The train was filled with those who wanted to reach as soon as possible the destination. The train ran continuously and they drank all the water, eat all the food, and in the end the fuel ran out. "We reached the communism" has announced the mechanic." It's true; said Pricop, everything was white, frozen and empty. The priest laughed, but he was convinced that Romania will not reach the communism. He was clandestinely to "The Voice of America" and was hoping that the Americans, as promised, will come. But they never came and the priest closed his eyes waiting for them.

Pricop was doing the shopping, and at the Armenian's shop at the corner of the street, he agreed to help the merchant with the maintenance of the shop and the yard work. The Armenian wasn't too generous, although after the departure of Jews he being one of the few merchants left, profited a lot. Many were saying that the Armenian enjoyed the hunt and deportation of the Jews.

Pricop was managing his money, collecting penny next to penny, thinking that one day he will be fortunate enough to set up a family. He put his eyes on Vasilica, but he did not dare to raise her eyes to her. One day he got courage to tell Mrs. of his intentions. Teodora promised that she will see what she can do. First she needs to find Vasilica's intensions. When Teodora found the right moment she asked her opinion about Pricop. Vasilica started to list all sorts of defects and imperfections, but when she noticed that Teodora had another opinion she slowed down, realizing that she had exaggerated.

"I never thought to marry," she said.

"It's good to think about." advised her Teodora. "You will be staying together in the house where the cabinet was. Times have changed and soon the special cabinets will be discontinued. We will keep house for our parents when they'll be real old and alone. Father Andrei is close to seventy years and can no longer serve Laza's people at the church for long. My parents are no longer in power and they will live here together with all of us. You will remain here as always, the one who will continue working as now. You would take care of kitchen and of children. Pricop is a very hardworking and the hardship through which he passed made him a better man and knowledgeable. My husband already thought to find him a job in the hospital or elsewhere. He will have a fixed program of work and a good payment. In his spare time he'll be in charge of the garden, courtyard, and some other things that he likes. You'll go together to the movies, walk in the park, to your parents and to the autumn fair.

Teodora's talk made Vasilica thinking if there are any qualities that she should discover at Pricop. When she called him for lunch she looked at him more carefully. She thought that the Lady already had a discussion with him, but the results were not yet visible.

Following Sunday after breakfast Teodora came in the kitchen and seeing the two of them said: "Today we leave with the kids to Laza, you two can go for a walk. There opened a new cinema, go to see a movie."

The two remained astonished. After Teodora left, Pricop got courage and asked: "it will be a good idea, what do you say, Vasilica?' She couldn't refuse Teodora's idea, and it seemed that also Pricop changed a little in the meantime. Not even his bold head wasn't the same, but there are so many men without hair and they don't care, some of them even look better bold. They went to the movie and this is how everything started.

After few weeks, on a Saturday afternoon Vasilica and Pricop, both very shy, bashful, went to doctor and Mrs. Manea, asking their approval to get married. They asked for a day off the next day to go to Gârceni to Vasilica's parents.

"We'll take you with the car", said the doctor.

The next day they left to Gârceni. The twins have remained at home; in the car wasn't space for all of them. They were promised that they'll be taken to the grandparents next weekend.

Vasilica's parents were pleasantly surprised by their daughter decision. They didn't have any objections, obviously. The marriage took place at Gârceni because Pricop didn't have any identity document except the certificate of birth from the town hall. There wasn't the time, it was not appropriate for a wedding. The Monetary Reform in August 1947 had left almost everyone without money, because the law imposed a fixed amount of money to be exchanged for each person. Manea family had enough cash, which he divided with generosity to parents or persons of confidence without asking anything in return.

Their treasure was still in the safe place, and served for the children's education. In fact the gold coins were Mihai's inheritance from his parents. Mihai, however, a generous soul who grew up in harmony with all his siblings, would have been always ready to share even a small piece of bread with his brothers.

Teodor and Teodora Manea were working at the hospital, and their efforts were very well reworded monetarily, which helped them raise and educate normally a family of four children. They didn't make any decision on when and how Mihai will receive his inheritance, but the doctor had a saying: "Everything at the right time".

And the years passed as it was yesterday...

*

August 1962. In Manea's family the life was quiet and total happiness. Ana and Mihai students in their 3rd year at the school of Medicine finished the last session with the best grades. They both were passionate about their future profession and during summer vacations they accompanied their father at the hospital, as real doctors. Dr. Manea was always the same, the best physician in the city. He helped his younger colleagues by promoting them, and everyone was very appreciative of his dedication. Teodora never made the case that she is the wife of the physician. Her modesty and moral integrity were qualities inherited from her parents, real farmers.

Gabriel's features didn't look as those of his brothers and sister (there was no way). On the other hand he borrowed their tenacity and application for science. He was admitted in the first year at Polytechnic Institute and was looking forward to start his studies. He remembered how at the first written exam he solved two problems in record time. When he went to give the paper work to the examiner, the Professor supervisor, believing that the young candidate gives up, unable to solve the problems, advised him to take his time, who knows, maybe the inspiration will come. Gabriel respectfully told the professor that he finished and he solved everything. The Professor, amazed, looked quickly over the paper, and out of curiosity, asked him what school comes from. "Mihail Kogalniceanu High School in Vaslui" he replied proudly. The Professor smiled, because he had heard of the fame of this high school which also Academician Gheorghe Vrânceanu attended. Gabriel was admitted being in the top three on the final list. When he looked at the list he started to read it from the bottom up, and stopped at about the seventh candidate convinced that failed. He went to his brothers who were waiting for him in front of the Xenopol's statue alerting them of his failure. The twins could not believe what their brother was saying and went together to look at the bulletin board. They began to read the list, of course, from the top down. There wasn't much to read because Manea Gabriel managed to be third on the list with an average of nine and sixty-two. They thought that their brother tried to kid them around.

Theodore Manea Jr. was in ninth grade at the same school where his brothers attended. His passions and inclinations moved to other areas: arts and foreign languages. The parents have proposed him to go to Iassy University at the foreign languages where there were so many possibilities for development in the areas which interested him. He refused, he said that he wasn't yet decided, but he wanted to fill up his hobbies by taking private lessons and learn himself.

Vasilica became helper nurse at the hospitals without special schooling, only with the Teodora's practical training. Pricop was totally changed, he looked better than when he was younger. He was a proud gate keeper in his post at the hospital. He learned to speak beautifully, he was carrying and civilized. He was helping and showed compassion to the sick people. When happened to meet some peasants from his village, his first instinct was to hug them, but then he refrained himself and helped them get to the doctor's cabinet, telling the doctor that the patient is from his village. The patient acquired extra confidence.

Pricop and Vasilica lived in the doctor's former cabinet, they had two rooms. The other rooms were kept for Teodora's parents, Catrina and Gică Rotaru. Father Andrei died, leaving behind only serene memories full of tenderness.

Since the twins had gone to Iasi, all the chores remained for the two younger brothers. And starting this fall only Junior will remain at home and he'll probably be overwhelmed by the love of his family. But, as always, the first love never gets forgotten and Ana and Mihai will keep their preferentially place. As future physicians, they felt the some sort of a pressure of the family love, and they tried very hard not to disappoint.

It was Saturday, a beautiful day of August, and Manea's family planned to go next day to visit Teodora's parents, who were in their 70s. Dr. Manea just finished a difficult surgery sat on a chair to rest for a few minutes. The patient, an old man with no education, had a stomach surgery. He disobeys the medical advice and in the evening, before the surgery, he had the imprudence to eat a portion of pasta from another patient. He did not mention to anyone about his feast at the dinner. After the incision, the nurses and doctors had to clean his stomach with tweezers all undigested pasta. The surgery was successful and the patient was sleeping peacefully without knowing what troubles produced. Manea's thoughts were interrupted by a discrete knock on the door. "Enter" answered the doctor. In office enters Pricop that there are three gentlemen who wish to talk to him, but they don't seem to be sick. For a moment Manea was thinking that they cannot be from Security. They came many times before asking him to become party members. But when he and Teodora became members of the party they ceased coming. At one time they wanted to take away the house in which was his medical cabinet, but now the documents were shown that the owners are Cârlig family and Rotaru family.

"Let them in" said the doctor. The doorman opened the door inviting them inside. The foreign persons introduced themselves: Flavius Solomon, Avram Leiba and Horia. After name, clothing and accent the doctor concluded that they are Jews. Luckily, he was touching the chair that provided some support; otherwise the doctor would have lost his balance. He felt some pinches in his heart. Ana or Mihai? In a split second, while the guests seated themselves he recompose himself and remembered some sequences of a documentary: images almost forgotten: the exchange of babies in the Isidor's house, Mihai sucking greedily at Teodora's breast, the desperation of Berta and Isidor to salvage their child by making the supreme gesture of swapping him with Teodora's deceased child and finally alienating him wrapped in a shroud following the Jewish Orthodox tradition. They wept, as the wrapped body was just their child. Then the sequences changed and at the forefront appeared Ana, which, in secret was his favorite child. The baby girl, small and skinny found in a basket left by her mother in desperation. This fast review made the doctor to disconnect from the environment for a moment. He excused himself, because he had a difficult operation and was a little tensed. To get a little more composed he rang the bell in the nurses' room. Very fast Teodora showed up; she was a little scared, not knowing what the rush is, and what's going on with her husband.

She made immediately a connection with the dream from the previous night, which turned out to be a nightmare. She dreamed that there was a large surface of water as in the biblical episode, and which was flooding everywhere. People, in desperation were running around as rabbits without legs and she holding Mihai's hand was looking for a place away from the water.

Paradoxically, the children weren't distressed; they were looking with interest at the new surroundings. Everything was as in a mute movie. Then the children disappeared and she woke up calling "Ana, Mihai where are you?" Manea woke up, and realized that she dreamed something unpleasant, and hugged her. "What connection can it be" asked herself "between her dream and the unexpected appearance of the three strangers?"

"Gentlemen", started Manea "I'm presenting to you my wife, Teodora Manea." Hearing the names of the three unannounced guests her heart also increased its rhythm, and pounded her chest. The doctor continued: "Please tell us what is the purpose of your visit."

First began to speak Flavius Solomon. His story was long. Berta's uncle former doctor from Botoşani was sent to Transnistria and had the luck to survive. After the war Solomon, Solomon left the country, in the U.S. A., where he had relatives and friends. He started all over and things went very well.

Avram Leiba, known as Lică, is an engineer constructor in Bacau and his wife Julieta is a teacher. Perhaps they will go to Israel. The young man Horia Solomon is Berta's young cousin. He finished his medical studies in London, and now he is a physician in Israel, in Tel Aviv.

"We all know the story of Mihai, a medical student, and now we came to see him", said Doctor Solomon. "With pleasure", said Manea while Teodora's face became livid, she clutched the eyes to not burst into tears. Manea knew that the students were leaving the hospital last so immediately went to look for them. No point to bring only Mihai because they knew that they're twins. Within minutes the twins, accompanied by their father entered the cabinet showing their curiosity and surprise by the presence of foreign people never seen before. The doctor felt powerless, exhausted and asked Teodora to disclose to the children their secret, which, without this visit would have went with them to the grave. Teodora Manea did not understand where and how their secret was deconspirate.

Flavius Solomon saw that the couple is not able to start this discussion and prepared his voice to start. Twins waited impatiently to find out what's going on. When Ana entered the room, the young Horia was attracted to her as a magnet. He never saw two eyes as beautiful, warm, and mysterious as hers. Ana felt his insistent look, and again, didn't know what the matter is.

"I am, dear Mihai, your maternal uncle", Solomon began. Mihai had never heard of Berta and looked astonished at his mother, whose voice vanished altogether. Each of the visitors said few things on the same line. Doctor Manea, while Teodora shed streams of tears, revealed Ana's identity. Teodora and Ana were embracing each other crying. After the secrets in connection with Mihai and Anna were unearthed everyone paused. Everything was on Mihai's shoulders; he was called upon to decide what he wants to do. In an instant, the student, who found out all these important details, gained a plus of maturity, revised his life so far: the childhood, the school, and the college period. He could not bring reproach or blame to anyone; on the contrary, life after the tragic event, about which he does not know anything, took place normally on a path lit by the care and love of those who surrounded him. Teodora is the best mother in the world. His father, doctor Manea example of dignity, diligence and devotion instilled qualities, all around. By not disclosing sooner a dramatic truth, spear them from a psychological trauma in their early childhood. Finding all of this now, at this time, the young students took the historical facts with a better understanding and realism.

While the Nazi stole from them with violence and bestiality their parents and family, in the same time the divinity rewarded them with the best adoptive parents and siblings. Ana looked at Mihai and desperately was begging in her mind, silently not to be disinherited from her the quality of being his twin. The deep silence was interrupted by a knock in the door. Manea opened the door, went out on the hall and asked the nurse not to be disturbed; because he has an important discussion with some people who came from Bucharest. He asked that the patients be directed to the doctor on duty. In the meantime Ana quieted for a moment; she felt that her psychic impulses reached Mihai who will forever remain her twin brother. She liked when everyone in high school and college called the Manea twins.

After these moments of thought, Mihai made a couple of small steps across the room and embraced his father, mother and sister and voiced his decision.

"Thank you, my dear, that you found me, probably was very difficult. I am very happy that I have other loving relatives discovered today. I have now two exceptional parents who saved my life risking their existence. They will always be my parents and Ana my twin sister. We'll visit you to meet other relatives, but we always return to our parents.

"Thank you, my dear, that I have found, it was probably very difficult. I am glad to know that I and other relatives as loving that I discovered today. But I have two outstanding parents who saved my risking life and existence. They will forever remain my parents and my twin sister Ana. We will visit you, to know other relatives, but I will always return to our parents. We would love to have you around for a couple of days, and I'm sure this is also my parents' wish." Then he kissed his parents and Ana. His sister looking Mihai in the eyes got the necessary impulse and repeated Mihai's gesture without saying a word. She kissed Flavius Solomon, Lică and Horia, who embraced her a little longer, feeling her inner vibration.

"It would be good" intervene Manea, "if the other two smaller not to be told anything yet about this matter. It counts very much the age of a child when is told certain things, which need to be judge in the context of history". All agreed with the proposal of a wise man.

Sunday's program was modified according to the new situation. The guests settle at the hotel and had a pleasant dinner at the restaurant. Two sons, Gabriel and Theodore stayed home. They had so much confidence in their parenting decisions that never asked for explanation.

The next day the same group went to Pungești at the grave of their ancestors. For the twins was the first visit to the cemetery. The tomb was well maintained and on the black marble stone was written the name Mihai. The twins touched the cold marble and felt invisible the connection with their forefathers and a new painful sentiment was born inside their young souls The next day, the newfound relatives went to Bacau with the promise to meet again soon. Horia wanted to remain one more day in Vaslui (only he knew why), but didn't get the permission from uncle Flavius. They took addresses, phone numbers, and each expressed the desire to see each other soon. Horia invited everyone to visit Israel on his expenses. He didn't know yet the state laws regarding the passports and visas for visiting foreign countries.

Monday at noon, after the guests had left doctor Manea received another visit from Security. To all the questions the doctor answered without hesitation that the foreigners were Lica and Avram, chief engineer at Construction Trust from Bacau and his friends who came from Israel to visit the tomb of their relatives from Pungești. The Security man believed him. The doctor, who was also the director of the hospital, through honest and professional performance managed to impose himself and so he didn't have too many enemies.

There were a couple of young people who were social climbers, but they kept the distance from doctor Manea. The doctor was very knowledgeable after so many years of study and experience accumulated, and combined with his natural goodness made him the best person to which all young people were coming for help and advice. He responded kindly to everyone, he was always present and willing to help the younger colleagues. At the large party meetings he never spoke, letting others to make proposals and engage in various party activities for their personal affirmation. Politics was not his forte point.

In a month Horia returned back in Vaslui for a whole week. He checked in a room at the hotel, meanwhile he learned that the Romanians are not allowed to accept foreigners in their homes. He brought from Tel Aviv a donation for the hospital of Vaslui. He spent most of his time with Anna and Mihai, his cousins. The arrival of relatives from Israel did not cause any surprises for children. The preference that Horia meets Ana and Mihai had a good explanatory reason: age and profession. Mihai noticed Horia's interest for Ana and from their behavior can be inferred that Ana's feelings were not indifferent for the young doctor. The twins left home together, but Mihai traveled through town inventing various businesses to take care of leaving them alone, the two lovers. And parents have noticed the attraction between Ana and Horia but do not sweat it, trusting in Ana's maturity and discernment.

*

In the autumn, when the classes started at colleges, three Manea students went to Iassy. Theodore Jr. started also his courses on the Arts and piano and foreign languages lessons.   In Vaslui there were professors for French and German, but he wanted to learn English as well. And so he was going twice /week at Iassy for English lessons.   His brother and sister started to attend also English classes, and the competition amongst the three of them was going on as usual.

Manea students lived in dormitories as Ana wanted.   The twins became familiar with the life on campus, the library study, the lecture hall, laboratories, and hospital practice.   They were delighted with their professors who were renowned in the medical field such as Dobrovici, Chipail, Oblu, Branzei, Lazar and others.

While the twins got used to the dormitories and campus life, harboring Gabriel was a problem.   When he entered a large hall with thirty beds, named bedroom, Gabriel had a shock. Ana and Mihai encouraged him saying that their dormitories are the same.   "The boarding life is very nice", encouraged him Ana.   "You learn so many things and stories of life across the country that you feel like in a theater, where you play a role. You will not have much time to stay in the dorm. You're going to courses, laboratories, the library and each minute of your time is precious".   Gabriel was not too convinced, and dropped his luggage on a random bed; he downloaded his cloth on some shelves waiting for other colleagues to meet in the afternoon. The new students, most of them freshmen arrived one by one, as they registered with the campus administration. There were four colleagues from Vaslui, all at the polytechnics but they ended up in different rooms.   The boys entered smiled, greeted, placed their things orderly in the spaces left, introduced themselves and the room became alive. Within an hour Gabriel found that the devil is not as black as they say. The students come from different places Suceava Pașcani, Bacău, Neamț, Bârlad, etc. all were cheerful and happy.   When someone entered the room felt the need to say something funny.   Those remained watchful, probably had some family problems in the family. Although the collectivization of the land and other goods was completed, the former rich families were not seen well.   In the same room there were children whose parents sympathized with other parties or had been in prisons. These children were marked, suspicious, cautious and ready to blow even in yogurt.   In a few years things were more settled and the young people imposed themselves through their work, making science not politics.

Once installed in their rooms the students went to the cafeteria. Gabriel found that although the food was not cooked like at home, it still had good flavor and taste. According to the plan, the twins came at the polytechnic's dormitory to take him out for a walk and show him around the campus. The walked slowly climbing the hill of Copou stopping in front of the University to admire the statue of Xenopol (Romanian scholar) and looked with admiration to the imposing building of University Ioan Cuza, the oldest University in the country, built in 1860. It resisted several earthquakes due to its solid structure and very thick walls. The polytechnic is in the same building on the right wing.

They continued their walk and entered in the Copou garden, stopping at the linden tree of Eminescu dressed in the autumn colors. Layer of fallen leaves were wet because the rain started. The whole garden was a symphony of fall colors. Some rays of the sun escaped through the clouds caressed their faces.

Manea brothers, enjoying the scenery, remembered the forest from the canton, their first contact with the nature. "Is the great pear still alive?" "But, what about the well's balance branch?" Is it still one piece or began to creak of old age?" They descended slowly, accompanied by the loud vibrations of the tram which was holding down its breaks. Each of them went to their 'home". Gabriel has found at his place the same pleasant noise. The youngsters were telling stories one at the time or all at once like a bunch of sparrows. But when one turned the lights off the noise went off too and all went to sleep. They woke up all at once, at six o'clock, running to the washers with white sinks side by side. Everyone was rushing to make to the class on time, at least in the first day. Most courses started at half past seven. Gabriel was summoned to the dean's office and told that his new function is the leader of the students in his group. It was his first victory in the battle of life. His rival, who was admitted the first on the list and who was the absolvent of the National Lyceum from Iassy was selected leader on a parallel group. This responsibility was a wake up signal. No more goofing as in the in the high school, here you must take things seriously. Shortly, he noticed that things weren't just so; the youngsters cannot stay for long without doing something strange. From the first contact with his group he informed them that the college requires that they should be on time to classes and not be absent from class without a serious excuse. He wanted his group to become a model of professionalism.

The first day passed like a white cloud, in a hurry. The next day he had a small incident, which in the end, eventually, turned into victory. They had hours in the electric laboratory. At the door Gabriel was greeted his colleagues with a smile and in the same time asking their names so to get to know each of them by name. In the doorway appeared a handsome young man, tall, with chiseled features. Gabriel didn't see him before, and asked him calmly: "What's your name?" "And what is your name? Replied the young man, "and please allow me to enter." Gabriel did not answer but took two steps back words leaving room for the newcomer to sit in a seat. The young man repeated: "I asked you to give me permission." But, seeing that the student does not move, he went around him directly to the professor's desk. "My name is Emilian Simionescu and I am your assistant professor for the he electrical machines." All sat dumbfounded because nobody would have thought that the young man could be already assistant professor and not one of their colleagues. "And what did you say was your name? He asked. "Manea Gabriel" answered the student with half of his voice. I had a colleague Manea from Bacau, are you related to him?" "No, I'm from Vaslui." Gabriel answered. "I figured it, that one was a smart guy. The break is over, let's get to work."

The lesson began with a description of the laboratory. Machines, motors, connecting wires, even the connecting outlets were presented; each of these was presented with extra information about who invented them, how and when. From the first contact with the young assistant, the students were impressed of his knowledge and his professionalism. What the students appreciated later at him, was the way in which he went from a joke to the scientific sobriety disconnected without breaking the flow of the lecture. The laboratory classes were attractive and no one was cutting them.

Gabriel ended his day, slightly annoyed. He remembered his expression "That was a smart guy."

The following classes brought the reconciliation. Simionescu treated him near as a peer, giving him the deserved respect. He was invited to the blackboard to write formulas and charts, draw diagrams, and praising him every time, and receiving always good marks.

During the breaks the assistant didn't go to the professors' room. He preferred to spend the time with the students chatting about everything. He was a master in telling jokes. Girls flock to be as close to him. They studied and came nicely dressed, but Simionescu treated them equally and none had any chance to conquer his heart.

In time, from various sources, they found more details about their young assistant.

The young assistant was a gifted child. He memorized alongside his older sister by two years in the first grade, all her lessons. The teacher, a friend of his father met him at home, and he was very surprised to see what the child knows. Ioan Simionescu was advised to enroll his son in the first grade, even if it was late November. Lia and her brother Emilian finished the elementary school with the highest marks. At Lyceum, Emilian caught the period when the Russian system was imposed. There were only 3 grades assigned for high school. He was admitted at the University when he wasn't even sixteen. He was gifted and industrious during college, and he finished with excellent marks. At the age when he sustained his master's other youngsters of his age were just enrolling at the University. He liked the research work but preferred to remain assistant professor at the University.

The assistant's scientific life was an inspiration for Gabriel, giving him a new impulse to dedicate himself to science. He didn't want to discontinue the competition with Ana and Mihai, who studied not for good marks but to acquire as many knowledge as possible.

Almost weekly, sometimes by rotation they went back home to Vaslui, where they've been spoiled with all sort of goof food, returning to Iassy loaded with a lot of goodness.

When the students returned to Iassy from vacations, especially after the Christmas holidays, the cold dorms immediately warmed up. They shared the food that the parents loaded them with their roommates. Those coming from Suceava were bringing pots of cabbage rolls, others brought mushrooms, specially prepared. There were pies with cheese, cabbage, potatoes, pumpkin, and apples. Everything was freshly home prepared by their parents and grandparents. If Gabriel wouldn't have listened to Ana he would have missed all of these and he would have never imagined how is the students' life on campus, the place where are born and die illusions, disillusions, dreams and aspirations, pains, pleasures, joys, all aligned like stars on the sky of our being enlightening our path.

In early December, in the afternoon, the administrator of the campus of medicine called Ana to tell her that a gentleman is waiting for her at the entrance. Horia dressed as an English lord, couldn't wait until the winter recess. The two have shook hands, and hugged with love. Their faces were glowing of joy, their feelings could no longer be held in check. They left together in the city to the hotel "Moldova" where Horia was staying. He remained in Iassy three days. For the day, evening, he arranged a joint program with the two brothers.

First thing in the morning, when the twins met Ana told Mihai everything. He said "It smells love to me", joked her brother.

Being Saturday, Horia, well-traveled, reserved a table for four for the afternoon. When they met in front of the restaurant, Mihai and Gaby embraced Horia and Horia kissed Ana's hand. No one, since now, kissed her hand with such tenderness. Her father kissed her hands differently, with paternal love. Their reunion turned into an evening of great celebration. Horia brought for Ana a bracelet which he fixed it on her hand, kissing her hand again. For next day, Sunday morning Horia proposed a joint program. Mihai and Gabriel found immediately that they have something else they need to attend to, excusing themselves, leaving the two lovers to spend the Sunday together. They understood and appreciated their gesture. Ana and Horia spent all the day in the city. Horia took her to the Hebrew cemetery, where Anna had never been. Holding their hands, they read the names of various people. The names didn't tell them much, but internally, secretly, they felt some sort of connection through invisible threads with these people. In the synagogue each of them inscribed in their hearts a wish. They looked each other in the eyes wondering if their wishes are identical.

In the afternoon they met again her brothers. In the evening Horia left for Bucharest and from there he would take a flight to Tell Aviv.

In the first Saturday spent at Vaslui, the youngsters told their parents about Horia's visit. Manea's heart was breaking at the thought that he might lose Ana. He loved her so much that he wanted to be near her all his life. Ana felt the need to confide in her parents, to ask for advice. She approached first Teodora for an intimate discussion between mother and daughter. The mother told her that in life she should follow two avenues: the profession and the love.

*

Another year passed. Another fall settles the old city of Iassy. The Copou garden was crying. The sky pulled down the heavy clouds, closer to the ground, which looked rotten of so much rain. The leaves of holy tree of Eminescu kneeled after long prayers in vain to heaven. The sun also scared of falling became red and it appeared smaller. Only the moon, the constellations were contemplating the Earth from their glacial empire. But the city retained the same charm, no matter what season was, rain, snow, or wind.

When the classes start, thousands of students were coming continuously as a river flowing from Copou to the old Lapusneanu Street until the Union Square, where the paths branch. The twins and Gabriel, as usual, arrived one the day before. Anna and Mihai had already their room ensured, every year the same.   Asked the administrator for a smaller room.. He agreed and Gabriel received a bed in a smaller dorm, only twenty beds. He arranged that some of his old friends be together. The rest were newcomers. Alex was also an electrical engineering student, but in another group. Alex was different, in the sense that he was very serious for his age. But his close friends discovered pretty quickly that this was just a thin curtain Colleagues found pretty quickly that this severity was like a veil drawn over an internal bonhomie.

Alex was gone from morning to evening, returning in the evening, after dinner in the cafeteria. That's true most of times he was seen in the library or laboratory. In few months Gabriel, who befriended him, learned that Alex was an Olympic in Mathematics for many years while in high school, and now he found an extra preoccupation which he loved: he was giving private lessons of mathematics. Tutoring other students was a pleasant job for him with double folded scope: to maintain his mathematical skills while earning some money. He had always money, but he didn't spend much as others did. His clothes were tastefully chosen. It is true that he had a nice figure that helped. He was tall, six feet past five and well built. By appearance seemed Nordic, blue eyes and blonde hair. Alex spent his summer vacations in Iassy until the admission exams at the university finished. No one of his students failed the admission exams at mathematics.

The second year brought other preoccupations. In general, in the first year the girls were struggling to strengthen relations and friends, while the boys were mostly observant, the solely preoccupied being studies, ensuring a safe and strong base. In the second year, also the boys began to move, still with caution.

The students' balls were their favorite pastimes. The most beautiful ones were organized by ISE Institute newly opened in new buildings, relatively modern. The parties were joyful, full of youthful exuberance, music and fun. During these parties many became friends and remained so for life. During the breaks between courses the students from the polytechnic Institute were often passing through the elegant corridor separating the rest of the University looking especially at the girls from philology, which in actuality were beautiful. Gabriel and some of his friends were doing this every week. In front of the entry in the amphitheater during breaks was a mixture of cardinals and swallows. So many girls were stealing your eyes and heart: Zefi, Stephanaia, Doina, Florentina Tudorita, Lia, Anca, Tina, Tatiana, all with beautiful names and faces. The boys from polytechnic usually were analyzing their appearances from bottom up and reached the conclusion that all had attractive legs, as if they were presenting a fashion show. Some of them besides beauty had also very good grades and were quiet selective regarding boys. The Engineering students didn't know as many lyrics from famous poets such as Blaga (at the time banned in textbooks and courses) or Eminescu but they were able to entertain any scientific conversation, which could not be translated the rhymes. In the following years many friendships were formed between these young students, which at first appeared incompatible.

Here, Gabriel met Tina, a junior student at Philology, romance languages. She had a statuary figure, blue eyes as violets, and curly hair. She was living in the dormitories "Justin Georgescu", and Gabriel sometimes passed by her dorm and invited her for short walks. The girl was cautious and suspicious in the relationship with him keeping the distance. Gabriel wasn't too insistent. He was only 20 years, and they managed to become friends, but only friends. Tina trusted Gabriel very much; many times she confessed to him many times her secrets, inclusive this one: The history class, under a zealous assistant professor organized a trip to Cluj taking a few students from her class. When they arrived in Cluj those from her class (romance languages), headed by Stelian and Julian, slipped away from the group and managed to get past the rest of the group. Their goal was to go to the Academy branch knowing that there they can find Lucian Blaga, the renegade and excluded from the university system because of his original philosophy. When he saw the group of students, the poet remained "mute as a swan". He exchanged with the group a few words of wisdom, then retired, being aware that his presence and the meeting would not make to any students from Iassy a service. The students from the romance languages, prospective teachers of Romanian literature, were very happy that they saw and spoke to the great Blaga. They didn't need anything else from the trip. Among them, in this group was, probably, a whistle blower who told to the assistant what happened. When they returned, the assistant went to the Dean of the Faculty of Philology, Gabriel Istrate, a great scholar, demanding that students who dared to see Blaga be sanctioned.

The Dean called the unruly students. Stelian, the head of the group confessed with sincerity that they had a meeting with "the poet of light". "Hey my children, did you really see Blaga, and how did he look like?" the Dean asked, disappointed that he was not among the students. Noticing that the Dean didn't show an adverse attitude, they told him in detail how did it happen and the meeting episode of the meeting with Blaga. But the exuberance was relatively short because their discussion was interrupted by a nervous knock on the door. The assistant from History entered the room; the Dean changed his smile and took a severe and harsh mean expressing his disapproval for such disobedience, as a conclusion of the previous conversation. He concluded sending them all out saying "I hope that this will not repeat." The assistant, badly would have liked to listen to the Dean sanctions, but he missed it because came late. "Comrade Assistant" said the Dean respectfully, "I think that we don't need to give big amplitude to this case. The students met Blaga unexpectedly, it wasn't something planned. If we make a big case out of this, you could be questioned that the group wasn't kept compact. This is not a case to exaggerate, and take into consideration bad intentioned gossips. I spoke to them very seriously, and I think that they understood. They all are very good students. This is my advice, but you can proceed as you think." The assistant left apparently satisfied. He was thinking that now when he place his candidacy for Assistant

Professor it may not be good to begin with investigations and security interventions.

The students who had the audacity to misbehave during that field trip thanked to the Dean, and studied seriously for the coming exam with the Dean. The regular good marks were not high enough to reward their acquired knowledge for that exam.

In fact, Tina trust in him, and the confession of this enormous secret gave him a lot of courage. He found from her colleagues that she obtained the highest marks at all the exams until then. Sometimes he thought that she knows too much and she reads too much for her age. He didn't have the courage to ask her if this wealth of knowledge was given to her by her parents. At the beginning of the second year, Tina told Gabriel that she has a lot to study, and she'll not have as much time for their walks.

*

The story about Tina, kept in secret, was quite similar to that of the twins in Manea's family, about which Gabriel didn't know about yet.

Tina's parents have been embarked in a death train. They were faced with a unique chance. The train stopped in the station at Roman, and people were freed temporarily by the Ladies from the Red Cross, while the train was cleaned, the sick and dead people were selected, and some Jews succeeded to flee from the gendarmes' watch and dispersed in all directions. Among those who escaped were also Tina's parents. Their luggage remained in the train. Sara, Tina's mother being pregnant, was wearing a large shall around her waist hiding cleverly a large amount of money to be used when necessary. Sara and her husband Ilie walked about an hour, stopping at the edge of the city in a very poor suburb. They went from house to house, trying to find some poor people, where they can stop for the night. After they knocked at the gate, a young woman with a colorful scarf over her head, opened. "We're Săbăoani" began Ilie , "and came to see the doctor, because my wife is pregnant and has some pain. A worker at the station told us to come here to stop for the night." "Yes, I know who you're talking about, please come in." Ilie didn't know anyone at the station; he just randomly introduced a worker into conversation, to be more credible. The interior of the room was modest. It seemed that the owners, newly wed, from the country side, recently moved to the city. Their assumption was correct. Shortly they found out that the young couple is from Roman village, and recently moved here, but shortly after they moved her husband was concentrated a couple of months back, perhaps he was sent on the battle field. "I didn't receive any news from him" she said. Sara, who became Zenovia, tired, but not sick as they said, asked permission to sit on the bed. Veta the woman's name, kindly, brought to her in a hurry a pillow from the other, unfinished room.

Veta put some potatoes on a pot to boil on the small stove. "I have to make some garlic to go with it" Veta said. "I don't have anything else to give you to eat." "Don't worry", said Ilie. "We'll give you some money, we didn't come to the doctor empty handed" and gave her a paper bill of thousand lei. "Oh, my Lord, what do I do with all this money?" "Go and buy something to eat, whatever you want, because Zenovia being pregnant needs some food. Tell to your grosser that some wealthier relatives pass by to see you." "I'll do what you say, because the grosser knows, I do have some money to pay him back." Please, pay what you have to pay him back, maybe Zenovia gets better and we don't have to see the doctor." "Thank you very much. Be it in the memory of our dead!" said Veta. Veta returned fast with a large loaf of bread, salty sardines, homemade salami, marmalade, and halva. She bought what she liked, thinking that her taste will please her guests. She wanted to give the change back, but Ilie refused. "We are very happy that you accommodated us, and we'll pay you more." "I feel better, said Zenovia, and I think that we can return home without bothering the doctor." "God bless", said Veta, "but please stay longer, until you'll feel much better. I am alone and with you here I feel so good."

They sat down and eat. Veta was delighting herself from the good food she bought, the two guests eat potatoes with garlic; the combination tasted good as never before. They slept well after the torturous time spent in the train, for two weeks, standing or lying down on the wagon's bare floor.

Next day the two women went shopping. Veta was the one doing the talking; Zenovia was trying hard to change her accent to a peasant one. "In Săbăoani, do you talk another language?" asked Veta. "Yes, we talk so and so" answered Zenovia.

They entered in the first shop and the merchant didn't notice that Zenovia, who didn't say anything, was Jewish. The two of them bought peasant cloth (just like Veta's), only the headkerchief were of different colors. Zenovia paid. "Where are you from? I didn't see you before?" asked the merchant. "From Săbăoani" answered Veta, proud of her cousin. "But in those places people wear different clothes", insisted the merchant. "Yes, but I didn't want to come to my cousin in those traditional cloth. But if you have any of those, I would like to see them. I need new cloth anyway." The merchant, very happy, that he'll make some sale, looked in a box, and pulled out all of its content. The two women selected a costume which wasn't different by much from the rest. The woman's costume had a black skirt, which ended with a red hem. At the waist line there was a shiny ribbon. The blouse was white made of cotton and adorned with large red flowers. "But for men do you have anything?" asked Zenovia; "I want to buy something for my husband. He wears the same size as you". The merchant found a man's tunic, shacked it, and put it on the chair. The costume with all its pieces wasn't too different from a peasant wear at the time: white pants and a shirt to the knee-long almost caught at the waist with a wide belt over which was laid right in the middle a belt decorated with silver rivets. The hats were made of cloth, short brimmed, they had one of the ordinary ribbon colored beads. For the holidays the lads were wearing a peacock feather. Zenovia took the feather too. "The total cost is two hundred" said the merchant, "but because you're Veta's cousin, I'll ask you for only one hundred and fifty." Therefore, due to Veta's relation, as relative, there came out some advantages. Ilie was totally surprised of Zenovia's idea, which turned out to be very useful.

When they decided to leave Veta insisted to remain longer; she got used with them. But the same day, at the gate showed up a young man, looking suspect, and who started to ask Veta about her visitors.

"They're my cousins from Săbăoani" started Veta. "Zenovia is pregnant and they came to see the doctor because she felt from the leader and she had pains. The doctor told her to rest for a couple of days and then to go home. They came to visit us in the past and nobody questioned me. Why? Now, because I am alone, because my husband has been taken to war, my relatives come more often to encourage me." Veta told to her guests about the discussion to which Ilie said jokingly: "They're looking, probably, for someone who escaped from prison or a dangerous thief. Why didn't you ask him in so I would too ask myself what he's looking for?"

In reality the police and soldiers were not allowed to say what happened, when they noticed that the death train, which was cleaned at the order of the distinguished ladies of the city, had less people, and started to panic. They became scared that they'll be punished for their lack of vigilance, and that's why the train was still stationed in the same place, hoping that they'll find some of those who escaped. The security decided, in secret, to send people and check around at the Romanian houses, if the escapee were hiding there. They returned, however, without finding anyone.

Zenovia and Ilie decided that they should leave that evening, but not to Săbăoani, as they told to Veta but to Botoşani, where they had some Romanian friends. Veta gave them two bags, because the cousins wanted to buy some food on their way home because in the village was hard to buy anything these days. Dressed as peasants they went with Veta to shop. They said goodbye to Veta and promised that they'll return to Roman again to visit her.

In train Zenovia and Ilie sat together with their bags full of food. Zenovia pregnancy wasn't advance, but she made sure that is visible at the ticket control and faking that she's asleep. The ticketing went without questions. At Botoşani they arrived early morning, took a horse carriage, and went to their friends who were still asleep. Their friends had a good laugh when saw them dressed in the peasant outfits. Their laugh changed in sadness when they found out what inferno they had to go through. In Botoşani the Jews have been deported in Transnistria, where a Romanian governor was installed. No one received yet news from those who left. The remaining Jews were living in fear. Sara's idea to dress in peasant cloth was ingenious and didn't create any suspicious.

After the war, in February 1945, when was signed the Decree which recognized the statute of all nationalities, the Jews regained their rights, and started to get integrated in the Romanian society devastated by the bellicose horrors that strained he whole world.

Sara and Ile recovered their houses but renounced to their shops, thinking that in those conditions many things will not stay the same. Ilie was a lawyer and found a job at a garment factory as consultant. Sara stayed home to raise their daughter Tina. When Tina was three years old, they decided to visit their "cousin" from Roman, who provided them shelter and saved them. But the street where Veta lived was full of bombing holes and none of the houses was standing. There were a lot of battles between the Russians and Germans, along with many bombs being dropped from both parts. They asked by passers if they know anything about Veta. Everyone answered that they don't know her. They returned to Botoşani very disappointed.

Gabriel's desire to get Tina's friendship didn't come true. Tina remained stubbornly motionless. Occasionally, he and others went to philology, but his heart was still at Tina.

Towards the end of the school year Ana asked him how's Tina. Gabriel answered that she's OK, but they didn't meet for a while because they are too busy. "I saw her one day on the street with a boy holding hands" said Ana. "That's possible, we didn't reach that phase, we're just friends."

In the third year Gabriel decided to devote his time only for study. All brothers started to take serious English lessons from the same professor. Ana and Horia were as engaged. They hoped that the uncle from America or Horia's relatives will facilitate a specialization.

The twins didn't want to separate but Ana was so in love with Horia that she would have went with him to the end of the Earth.

The parents got used with the fact that Ana wants to leave the country and could not oppose her dream.

Gabriel came with the idea that he wants to attend courses from the Economic Sciences college. He spoke to his mentor Assistant Professor Simionescu to see what is his take regarding this idea. The assistant, who was working at his Ph.D. thesis, encouraged him that in his career of engineer or professor it is good to get knowledgeable in economy, accounting, commerce, and banking. Horia started to prepare himself for the admission exams. At mathematics he didn't have problems. He liked the Geography and the book of political economy was small, not even two hundred pages, and with his strong memory he would have absorbed in a month most of what was required. He told to the twins his plan and they also encouraged him. The only problem was the money. It wasn't too much, and because all had scholarships, he hoped that the parents will help out with his taxes, due to the fact that the second specialization is not tax free anymore. When he started the third year at Polytechnic he was first year at the Economic Sciences. All his roommates from the first year of college remain together. Some extra high drawers appeared in the room. They didn't have yet a refrigerator, even if their lunches together were still going on almost every week.

The fall passed, the winter holidays came, and all left campus to stay with their relatives at Christmas and New Year. After more than a week home, with good food and relaxation all the students from Manea's family finished the exams with excellent marks. Room 14 didn't have anyone who lost an exam. Gabriel had two sets of examinations: at Polytechnic and at the Economic Sciences. Some of his exams at the Economic Sciences have been equated with those from the Polytechnic. For him the third year at the University passed faster than the other prior two. He would start his fourth year relaxed. Gabriel absorbed a lot of theory, only the labs and practical work with all its diversified forms was as a sack with a broken bottom. He changed the library with the lab. He was passionate for electronics, the science of the future, followed by other new topics such as computer programming and encryption.

His uncle from America and Horia from Tel Aviv were sending magazines of medicine for the twins and electronic for Gabriel. Their knowledge of English helped them a lot now, and they became fluent in reading and conversation. Gabriel was sharing his magazines with his assistant, who in the meantime finished his Ph.D. theses with an invention in the high voltage electricity, which didn't find an applicant locally, but it was well received in other developed countries.

In one Sunday, when he was working in the lab with the assistant, all of a sudden the door opened without noise and he saw a beautiful and well-dressed lady. She wasn't one of the students he knew from Polytechnic, who were trying through all methods to attract the assistant's attention. Emilian presented her as being Mira, student at the Textile Industry College, where the assistant had some lab classes. They left together leaving Gabriel submersed in his lab work. Next day Gabriel couldn't abstain not to tell is colleagues what a beautiful friend the assistant has. The girls were terrible disappointed; their hopes of getting the assistant's attention were lost forever.

*

The medicine school from Iassy was in a festive setting. The young students, who days back were shaking of emotion at the admission exams, were now, after six years, doctors. The time was generous with them; their faces became beautiful and their bodies stronger. More maturity was present on their overall presence.

The yard of the school was full of young absolvents, but not only. There were parents, and relatives with flowers, enjoying the time of their festive meeting. The absolvents, doctors ready to obey Aesculapius (the God of Medicine), were dressed with their traditional togas and quiet emotional. Some were happy that the studies finished, others concerned that there is still so much to learn all their life.

They received the new assigned places of work. Ana wanted to specialize in cardiology; and she was assigned at the Parhon hospital. Mihai wanted to be a surgeon, but remained assistant professor, thinking that in a couple of years he'll follow up on his desire accordingly.

That summer was the last vacation when all brothers will spend it together. The parents made a big effort to make every day as pleasant as possible - the thought that Ana will leave them was killing them.

"I love him mother, and you told me sometime, that the most important things in life are the profession and love; I have them both, and I want to save them." Teodora hugged her and agreed with her decision. The same did Manea.

Every afternoon they visited the Jewish cemetery from Pungeşti and read with loud voices the names engraved in the old marble plates: Isidor, Sara, Erna, Tibor, Joseph, Roze, Gabor, Rita, Mihai.

Another afternoon they spent at the canton, where they found a new ranger. When he found out who are they, the ranger and his wife invited them inside and opened a jar of wild raspberries comfiture with cold water. When they left she offered them many jars with homemade jam from the forest berries, and bitter cherries. They linger a little while under the pear and talked to it "You know uncle pear, I will leave and maybe I'll never see you again" Ana said sadly. She broke a few leaves and saved them. Uphill they collected slightly yellowed green acorns and clipped them on her hair. From the canton they went to Gârceni taking with them a bouquet of wild flowers and forest's grasses. They arrived when the sun was ready to set. The grandparents Catrina and Gică instantly became ten years younger when they saw the house full of grandchildren. The knees and backs didn't hurt anymore; they moved fast around. When the old ages saw so many doctors around went away fast through the back door. "What does it hurt grandma?" "Nothing." "What does it hurt grandpa?" "Nothing." Only Ana's soul was hurting, and for this kind of pain the medicine didn't find a cure.

They returned to Vaslui after three days, fresh as the morning dew.

Gabriel left for Iassy with Teodor Junior who had the entrance exam. He enrolled at the philology college for the English-German section.

The two brothers lived in Gabriel's room. They found there Alex, who usually didn't leave until the students he prepared received their results.

Teodor was to get examined in writing and oral at three subjects: maternal language, English, and German. This year it happened to be a large number of students enrolled for admission examination, something like six students for one place. When the results have been posted, Teodor showed maximum grades for foreign languages.

While the two brothers were away, in Vaslui Ana's fiancée arrived. Also, in this time Ana and Horia got married. They left together to Bucharest to confront the autocracy of documentation; Horia set in motion his entire network.

Relatives from Israel, America, and Switzerland worked together in the background. In a month Horia Ana received their approval, passports, legalization of diplomas, certificates, and everything they needed that Ana may leave the country permanently, by marriage.

Teodor and Teodora had shed rivers of tears, only at night, because during the day they had to keep a happy face. Ana could not take any memorabilia, but Teodora gave her a small ring carefully saved in its velvet box from Julia.

Life flows on without calendar. Things, in general, get broken, get life, or die without our will. The three guests who came to Vaslui, years ago, to take Mihai, left only with Ana about they didn't have any knowledge, or they knew something, but didn't talk about.

At the airport Ana was accompanied by parents and Mihai. The young Mrs. Solomon made a big effort not to cry. These were tears of pain combined with happiness and she didn't wanted to waist them. She never flew before, but she handled very well the fear. She held her parents hands kissing their pale and cold cheeks. The parents stopped crying. Mihai entertained Horia talking about Ana: "She is smart, courageous, very sensible, please take care of her; we protected her as a snow flake."

The speakers announced that the passengers for Tel Aviv flight are invited in the waiting room. Horia embraced his in-laws, and Mihai. Took Ana's hand, now Mrs. Solomon, and waived goodbyes.

From the general waiting room the parents were looking at the plane, which slowly, slowly departed to the takeoff line. In other few minutes it accelerated and detached from the ground as a huge silver bird, which took Ana with it.

Teodora closed her eyes, leaning on Manea. For a second, in her brain appeared the old image of the bombing plane that flew above Vaslui and the bombardment in which Julia died. "Mother, you're OK?" asked Mihai. "Yes, it passed. Let's go."

The house in Vaslui, which not too long ago was full of children, now was deserted and cold. Sometimes Teodora or Manea heard echoes of children's voices, which filled the atmosphere, with their healthy laughs. Vasilica was missing the four doves that she helped to grow up. Pricop attending the garden, was seeing through the branches of the trees a child of four who collected he fall colored leave for Vasilica to save them

From Israel she sent back very detailed letters and photo albums. Very often she made phone calls. She sent frequently specialty magazines, samples of the latest discoveries.

The Clinique at which Ana worked now was in Tel Aviv. It was richly equipped. There was no comparison with the similar Clinique in Iassy.

She attended a specialization seminar in New York. Uncle Flavius took care of her accommodations. He wouldn't accept another way. She had a chauffeur who took care of her transportation. The old doctor wanted that his niece feel good and have a nice experience in New York.

There was great love and care that she felt from her uncle's part; she thought that there should be some other secrets and maybe she is for real his blood niece. The curiosity was so great that in one evening she had the courage to ask uncle Flavius if three is something else she doesn't know in relation to her roots. The uncle, maybe knew, or maybe not, but didn't want to tell her anything. "Dear Ana, you are my niece and your children will be my nephews through blood. Israel is your land. In regards to Mihai, even if he'll not leave in Israel, he'll be able to travel everywhere in this world, and he'll enjoy our help, because the blood cannot be changed in water." "In Romania, currently is popular the saying that expresses the selfishness very well "to die the neighbor's sheep, while the Jews think and help each other and said "to live the neighbor's sheep too."

Ana's time was scheduled minute by minute, but she found time to visit the Holocaust Museum. The girl kept a daily diary about the time spent there. The journal starts June 12, 1942 and ends August 1, 1944, when the Gestapo discovered the two hidden families and deported all of them to Bergen-Belsen camp. The girls didn't survive the treatment in the campus and died two months before the liberation of Holland in March 1945. The journal remained a written account of the tremendous hardship she had to face. It has been printed in many languages, and read by many people all over the world.

Through the numerous exposed things at the museum there is also an album discovered, incidentally by Lily Jacob, who survived the Auschwitz. The photographs snap shots have been taken by the Nazis, showing the tremendous torture scenes of Jews.

During the visit at the museum the young Dr. Solomon was re-living a strange sentiment which she felt back few years, in the Jewish cemetery from Pungeşti: a brisk slide on the history steps and a return in time, with three thousand years back with the red eyes and transfigured look, in front of her was projected the biblical gesture of Moise, who parted the see in two, made such that the sons of Israel will safely pass towards the Saint Land. The Holocaust Museum added a new and important page to the spiritual knowledge of the young doctor.

At the Clinique, the lectures were winding up, but Ana very energetically, made all the efforts to assimilate all the details related to her profession. At the last exam, she received the maximum mark. The professor in charge with the specialization proposed to her to remain at their Clinique, in a position of assistant professor, and cardiology doctor. She politely refused the offer, telling them that she had family in Tel Aviv. But she jokingly, promised to the professor that she'll send her twin brother, professor assistant from Iassy, in Romania. The professor was enchanted and said that he'll wait for him.

Returned back home, they started to work on the process of inviting her parent to Israel. In those days travelling abroad from Romania wasn't an easy proposition. In few months Teodora and doctor Manea received their passports. While waiting they documented and learned few things about Israel. This was their first trip outside the country. The emotions were complex, but at the thought that they'll have the opportunity to hug their daughter nothing was difficult.

They wanted to visit Jerusalem, the city of legends and rich history. Their plan was to stay for two weeks. Next in line that planned such a visit was Mihai. Again, in those days the law didn't allow that a family travel together.

Most people were wandering how come they can travel? This meant that they had relations. The truth of the matter was that they, indeed, had relations.

The parents returned from their visit, and from there on, they travel back and forth for many years. When Ana gave birth to their grandson, only Teodora went and spent several months, taking leave without pay from the hospital. Doctor Manea couldn't stay for so long away from the hospital.

Mihai received a fellowship from New York, exactly from the Clinique at which Ana had her specialization; it meant that uncle Flavius didn't forget Mihai. The young researcher, manager over the projects, collected enough material for his doctoral thesis. He was on an excellent path.

He travelled frequently to congresses, not only in Israel but in many other countries, and every time he returned to Iassy. His book "The pathology of the rhythm disorders" translated in English brought him a good notoriety.

When Ana left she took something from his being, because despite of all the developments that followed, they remained twins; because this was the way they were raised and educated. The twin sentiment wasn't altered, and didn't die. They continued to work together in research of the diagnostic of the cardio vascular diseases.

Gabriel was in his last year of studies, preparing his license's thesis. His topic was selected such that it will combine the electronic with the studies from the Economic Sciences, where he was in his third year. He consulted his mentor, the assistant, who finished his doctorate at the age of 27 and became Professor.

The time was galloping, extremely fast for all. He sustained his thesis, and all the exams. Mihai was preparing his doctoral thesis and was waiting for all the family at Vaslui. They gather all at home, but they felt that something is missing – Ana's departure affected not only the parents but also the boys. Her laughter, her piano playing, her comments on read books, philosophical discussions, all were closed in photos carefully arranged by Teodor in a photo album. On the cover of the album was written: ANA.

Teodor junior, who used to be the joker, and present everywhere for entertainment, was staying in his room surrounded by dictionaries and books; it seemed that he forgot that he's in vacation. Finally, he confessed that he has an exam left for the fall session with Professor Jean Livescu. A colleague, who didn't study for this particular exam, thought that she can copy at this exam. She sat at the table next to him with her inspiring papers. After she finished copying, placed the inspirational papers under the table. The professor observed what's going on and without too much research or discussion he marked her and Teodor's examination papers, and took away the hidden papers from under desk. Teodor left the room without commenting and didn't show at the oral examination. The girl tried to beg for forgiveness. This incident made Teodor to lose his scholarship for the following year.

Gabriel Manea and Alex Simionescu have been assigned assistant professors. As assistants they had the option of choosing accommodation in the newly constructed building reserved only for academics. The two of them were overly excited and agreed to become roommates. Both were seriously involved in research; there were no prospects that one of them would marry soon. Their bachelor status was in danger because in the same building were plenty of girls, single assistants, some of them very attractive. Among them there were two who lived together in room 16, second floor. One of them came from Timisoara University, and the other graduated from Iassy University.

Alesia graduated with top marks from the German section at the University of Timişoara. She was born in Rupea and wished to receive a position in Braşov, Sibiu, or Făgăraş, only to be in the Transylvania area, where she was born and grew up.

The only convenient place, in terms of scientific and professional point of view, shown in the list, however, was Iassy. Many graduates wanted a place in Iassy but their average at the graduation wasn't high enough.

With tears in her eyes, Alesia accepted the position of assistant at the University of Iassy. She knew very little about the capital of Moldova and in addition it seems to be so far, like at the end of the world.

In college she had some colleagues from Moldova but she didn't stick to them. Even in her huge dormitory were three girls from Suceava, but there was very little dialogue. In time she became used with their usual speech and behavior, and even listened to the picturesque stories of Moldovian girls. She started to believe that the parts where Bistriţa and Siret rivers were flowing, and the ground trodden by the bison's hooves, is a repository of folklore and ancient culture insufficiently explored. The Moldavian spirituality is very rich. Examples are musicians Ciprian Porumbescu, George Enescu, Mihai Eminescu, Mihail Sadoveanu, Stefan Luchian, Nicolae Iorga, Octav Onicescu, Gheorghe Vrancearu, and many others. These names weren't sufficient to determine the young absolvent from Transylvania, raised in German style to leave those places without sadness. The road to the Moldavian capital was accompanied with tears. From her colleagues from Suceava she retained: "All bad toward good". This is all she had in her brain in those sad moments.

From Timisoara to Iassy the travel felt endless so she made a stopover in Bucharest where her uncle lived. Her uncle stoically faced the havoc of war, the post-war German prosecution in Banat, gave her a realistic thinking, and encouraged her to go without fear to Iassy. Her uncle's advices inspired her some optimism. The travel from Bucharest to Iassy wasn't as painful, even if the train was slowly moving as a snail, irritating the nerves of those who were in rush.

The Iassy station, old and dark gave her a desolate image. She took the electric tram, which was also old. It crossed the city until the Cuckoo Market.

Alesia didn't carry too much luggage, and preferred to walk to the hotel in the United Plaza. She took a room for a night. She could not go directly to the Dean immediately from the train. Many others did. Next day, she dressed nice and appropriate and went to the Dean's office, where other new hire were waiting. Her appearance was immediately noticed. She was like a statue in movement walking on the hallways with a gazelle's elegance. She greeted everyone around as she knew them for long. A young lady asked her where she comes from. The name of Timişoara had a special resonance. Finding that her specialty is German languages, her colleagues understood why she studied at Timişoara.

When came her turn to see the Dean, she felt a special emotion. Nevertheless, she stepped in fully confident. She said "Hello" and gave her assignment papers to the Dean. The Dean, a man passed over fifty, was still an attractive and likable man. He stood lustfully and showed her the seat. During their conversation he enjoyed learning that she will teach German, because he was a professor of German and spent a year of specialization in Germany. This opportunity was the luck of his life, because he found that he has a serious disease about which he didn't know; the Germans treated him using the most advanced medication and he was cured. He returned home perfectly healed, and with a bag of knowledge.

The discussion in German was pleasant, the Dean emphasized that the future engineers need to become fluent in German due to the economic relations between the two countries. She received the approval to get a room at the University's non-family building. "How was it?" "How was it?" the torrent of questions came from those waiting to have the starting interview with the Dean. "Good" answered Alesia, "I received the approval for a room in the non-family quarters." One of the girls, nice looking and very sociable introduced herself: Liliana Pancu. "I am Assistant at the chemistry department and I will live in the same building. If you want we can walk there together."

The girls stayed there for a couple of minutes and then they left together descending on the Lăpuşneanu Street, until the hotel, where Alesia left her luggage. The luggage was small, no heavy to be carried. At the building, the administrator gave them the room 16 on the second floor. The events from the first day transformed positively the new assistant's spirit. She renounced for a moment to the idea of an eventual exchange of the place of work with one in Timişoara. The time was passing fast, the city became increasingly more attractive and the colleagues of her generation were warm and hospitable; all of these weakened the prejudice with which she came from Timisoara.

The room in which they lived was small but better than the large dormitory of 25 beds from Timisoara's campus. The furniture in the room was standard: two beds with a night stand, a large closet for cloth, a desk and two chairs. At the end of the hallway was the common kitchen.

In the months that followed Alesia and Liliana decorated the room in their taste. The bought new bedding, blankets, pillows, a small rug with geometrical motifs in pastel colors, drapes, table cloth, and many other objects to make their room pleasant to live in. A large painting on the white wall was catching the eyes. The scene was a mountain and a river with transparent silvery water which was letting the eyes to search for the fish moving up stream. Several old goblets completed their arrangement. The table cloth made of heavy silk, with rich embroidery on the edges was let hang to cover half of the skinny legs of the table. On each chair was a small pillow covered on the same fabric as the bed covers. On the table was a large vase of heavy glass with deep incrustations to imitate the crystal.

On the same hallway, on the second floor, were living not only the young assistants but also those who were around for a couple of years like heads of the research labs. Two couples married in the summer, but continued to live in the same place. Liliana finished her studies in Iassy, and therefore, she knew very well the city. She had plenty of friends and was never alone.

The fall season was long and beautiful. Alesia and Liliana were on the go through the city visiting monuments, Gardens, the Central Library, the Dosoftei Literature Museum, the cultural palace, the Three Hierarch's Church, and others. Every day the city opened under Alesia's eyes as an album in movement, in color, alive, and colorful voices with an amalgam of accents which irresistible attracted her. The beautiful city with old traditions as Timisoara and Brasov, which she loved so much, started to fade in the shadow of her memory re-invigorated by the seven-hills of Iassy with their archaic inscriptions, piously buried in the dust of history.

On the second floor's hallway, Alesia's steps were under observation. One of the assistants from the Polytechnic found out the schedule of Miss Alesia and made himself incidental need to see or to listen to the rhythmic music of the high heels style Louis Quinze, in vogue at that time.

In a relatively short time the residents from the building started to know each other, and greeted each other. The free time started to be compressed, then expanded to attend the Philharmonic Hall or the National Theatre.

Gabriel and Alex have not remained indifferent when the new blonde, brunettes, or brown assistant ladies showed on the building. "Did you see what legs of a gazelle the German assistant has?" asked Gabriel one day when they both were following Alesia. "Yes, but not only legs" answered his friend. "I think that we should invite them one Saturday evening at Bucium, at the vineyard." Gabriel agreed, and one day they both discretely knock at door of room 16. The girls were in the room, but the boys didn't want to enter; only made them the proposal to spend some time together. The girls accepted without reservation. Until that Saturday the group became larger because the boys didn't want that their getaway be to intimate.

Their get together in small or large groups continued all fall. After few moths the group started to partition in pairs. Gabriel liked Liliana and Alex liked Alesia, but neither of them were in rush. All had seminars to prepare, and devoted time and attention to the scientific details. Gabriel didn't forget what a fantastic impression made on him the assistant Emilian Simionescu from the first day, and he became a model to follow.

The two colleagues were preoccupied to find the domain and the scientific direction on which their thesis will be directed. In function of the topic, they will be given a scientific coordinator.

The girls were not in any hurry for their doctorate, but wanted spiritual relaxation, and intellectual enjoyment: concerts, theater. The National Theater from Iassy had a rich repertoire and much appreciated by spectators. The great actor Miluță Gheorghiu, whose interpretation of Madam Chirița of Ioan Luca Caragiale was the delight of the public. The Philharmonic theatre from Iassy had deep roots in the Romanian culture, if we consider the philharmonic dramatic conservatory which opened in 1836, re-opened after the war giving weekly concerts of the best quality. The permanent director of the philharmonic hall was Ion Buciu invited great musical performers from abroad and from all everywhere in the country. At Iassy were invited to perform Ion Voicu, Valentin Gheorghiu, Ştefan Ruha, Madrigal Chorus, under the baton on Marin Constantin, and other renown musicians. When the Beethoven IX symphony was played always on the directing podium was Iosif Conta. Alesia and Liliana didn't miss any of the concerts. Sometimes, they invited also friends with lesser affinities for musical arts. The engineers had found an explanation: the science helps them to make an objective selection. Only the mathematician-poet Ion Barbu discovered the highest point in the Universe where the science of mathematics meets the poetry.

Gabriel, in the meantime, took his license at the Economic Sciences. His finals were extraordinary, and his professors offered him the option to take the associate assistant position with them. But he asked for time to think about. "I know that I don't know much" was thinking many times the assistant, frustrated that could not grasp fast enough everything that he wanted, because the science was evolving so quickly, with huge laps, while the brain has its own rhythm.

*

The summer vacation brought many changes to Manea family. In the eve of Mihai's departure to a conference in Paris, he got to know a doctor from the Fundeni's hospital who was going also to the conference. Hey met in a way as the destiny was following a precise path. The young doctor Raluca Vancea was going for the first time to Paris and she was a little emotional about this. She found out that a colleague from Iassy was going to the same conference. She contacted him by phone, and asked how he looks like so she'll recognize him when he comes to the Otopeni airport.

When she arrived at the airport, she looked around but no one fit the description given by Mihai. She sat on a bench, reserving the seat next to her with a magazine. When Mihai entered, an internal feeling told her that he must be and she waived at him.

Mihai had the same feeling. He went to her and introduced himself. "Mihai Manea", "Raluca Vrance" she answered with an affectionate smile. Seated next to each other, they started to talk as they knew each other since the making of the world.

Mihai, who was almost 28 years old, didn't have any intimate girl friend with which he could start a long lasting relationship.

At the University Manea twins were together everywhere. The colleagues who courted Mihai were kept at the distance by Ana, who didn't accept a separation from her brother. Maybe in her soul was also a bit of egoism which was generated by an exaggerated affection. The same phenomenon happened with Mihai, who considered that the boys, who tried Ana's friendship, were not at her level. Each twin became a protective angel for each other. Obviously, all of these had a reason; their career was on the first plane.

When in Ana's life appeared Horia everything took another direction. Mihai accepted him from the first moment, intuitively thinking that the two will make a good couple.

Becoming doctor, the girls approached him more often than before, but he remained conservative filtering everything not only with the heart but also with the rational. Ana remained for him the ideal feminine model and almost no one could be as her. Teodora, his mother, also represented a reference point difficult to match.

Seated near Raluca, about which he didn't know anything, Mihai seemed confused. Physically she didn't look as Teodora, neither as Ana, nevertheless there was something that made her attractive to him, and he let himself pleasantly seduced.

By the time of departure they confessed to each other so many little things, which made each of them, believe that they knew each other from another world. As medical doctors, though they didn't accept the re-incarnation theory.

Between the Earth and sky the duration of the flight seemed very short, and there was not enough time to finish each other's confessions and scientific conversations.

At the airport, in Paris, a representative from the Conference was waiting for them. He noticed that the two were almost a couple; nevertheless he asked if they want separate rooms or an apartment. Mihai looked at Raluca letting her to decide. "Apartment" was Raluca's reply.

When they took the apartment's keys, Raluca felt obliged to explain herself. "Please excuse me, Mihai, for the decision I took, but I am afraid to stay alone in a room, in Paris. I promise you that we'll be two serious friends." Mihai tried to understand Raluca not having other motives. She decided that the bedroom will be his and she'll take the couch in the living room. Each one in their own room unpacked and prepared their things for the next day. After a French bath Raluca discretely knocked at Mihai's door and said "Good night." And then went to sleep. She slept very well until the morning. Through Mihai's mind were rushing, for a while, various thoughts; some fantasies, but in the end he fell asleep too.

In the morning, nicely dressed, and still very professional they left together with the doctor who greeted them at the airport to the conference place. Their presentations were scheduled for the next day, and therefore they had time to get used with the rhythm imposed by the French organizers. In the first day Mihai had an intervention appreciated by his colleagues. Raluca was listening to her new friend, enjoying his success. The two of them were considered a couple and they did act accordingly.

In the evening they visited the city of light comparing it with the cities in Romania, which were kept in total dark.

Second evening between the two partners of the apartment started a light connectivity. Each of them recited with loud voice their communication, and applauded each other for the performance, and then each of them went to sleep.

Their presentations were very well received. Mihai bought for Raluca an orchid. To celebrate their success they bought a bottle of champagne. Each drank a glass, and saved the rest for the next evening. Raluca went quietly to sleep wishing as usual "good night" to Mihai. Mihai was again caught by surprise, not knowing what to believe. They'll remain to the end only cohabitants of the apartment? In any event he thought to make a chivalrous gesture that could lead to thawing relations. Stopping her in the doorway gently kissed her hand affectionately. The girl didn't remain indifferent and returned the gesture with a kiss on his cheek. But then immediately she closed the door behind her.

Third day they were more relaxed around town holding their hands. Mihai did some shopping and bought some batch shampoo with a nice fragrance. In the evening they drank drop by drop the left over champagne.

Mihai prepared a surprise. In the large bathtub filled with water she dropped some shampoo which transformed the water in a fragrant seductive sea of snowy foam. When Raluca saw the bathtub full of foam couldn't resist and pulled off her dress and hastily threw as a child in the bathtub spewing water everywhere. "You can do so too" suggested the girl. Mihai could not refuse such a proposal. In the bathtub they played as two young children in the snow. Taking advantage of the excitement of the game Mihai like accidentally freed Raluca's bra letting her young breasts to mingle with the foam. The play went on and covered by the foam she looked as a nymph borne from the foamy waves of the sea.

After the bath Raluca inadvertently hit the big bed of the bedroom, leaving Mihai to decide where to sleep. Later in the night, when the girl went into the bathroom, the bath water flowed out leaving witnesses underwear stifled covered in the perfumed foam that didn't fade away yet.

The Parisian morning light crept discreetly through the blinders of the window, resting for a while over the bodies of the two lovers after a fulfilled desire.

"Good morning my fairy, I love you, I love you, I love you!"

*

Mihai's doctoral thesis was ready and the Professor coordinator needed to coordinate the calendars of all the members from the doctoral commission and fix a day for presentation. One of the members in the commission was from Bucharest.

At the beginning of August, the whole family, except Ana, gathered again in Vaslui.

Mihai was preparing the terrain for Raluca's arrival in family. She will be their guest and she'll stay in Ana's room which was kept intact since she left. Raluca could not stay more than two days, which would be enough for Manea's family to get introduced to Mihai's girlfriend, and get a glimpse at their possible daughter in law.

Vasilica devoted all her talents and energy in preparing everything that could be Moldovian tradition. Pricop was moving as fast as he could through stores ad markets buying things from the lists prepared by Vasilica.

Teodora and doctor Manea were working normal hours at the hospital, while Vasilica was in charge of everything..

Gabriel was in his room working his ciphers, alarm systems, bells and other accessories for his electronics projects. Teodor junior was writing poetry. He received already several prizes "Young talents" and the "Visionaries". The magazine "The New Iassy" published his poems and fragments of historical stories. He was in his last year of studies. Gabriel saw him many times with beautiful girls, but always with a different one. He didn't find yet a steady friendship.

Mihai felt very emotional, he was moving objects from a place to the other, or when he passed by the piano, was trying several tones. It was Saturday; Raluca arrived with the train around 5 PM. The family had just one car, which most times driven by doctor Manea, and so Mihai was forced to go to the station with his father. They waited for her on the terrace because there the heat was cooler. The beautiful girl mad a great impression to doctor Manea; she was mannered, natural, and very open. Al expected that a girl who comes from Bucharest would be more temperamental. But wasn't so, Raluca made an excellent impression and captured everyone's attention from the first moment. Raluca liked the house and highly appreciated the hospitality in Ana's room, about Mihai told her many things.

Sunday morning the young pair walked through the city public garden renowned for its beautiful roses. The lunch was served on the terrace, and was very festive. They talked, eat and laughed a lot. Raluca left to Bucharest with the evening train leaving behind her perfume and many hopes. She passed with high marks the family "examination" and she could become Mrs. Manea anytime; the decision belonging to the two. There was only one drawback: Raluca was working in Bucharest at Fundeni's Hospital, a position too good to change. But they agreed that after Mihai's doctoral thesis he'll look for a position in Bucharest.

*

At the Polytechnic's dorms, during Gabriel absence, Alex announced his engagement to be married with Alesia. After marriage they'll be moving in a larger room dedicated to couples. Gabriel didn't want another roommate convinced that would be impossible to find a friend as good as Alex. Teodor Junior, in the last year at the University decided that along with Gabriel to take apartment in the city. Luckily, they found a room in Păcurari, very close to the University, in a new building, built by the Factory of antibiotics. The owner was an engineer, unmarried, decided to sublet part of his apartment, so he'll not be alone. He liked the two young men and rented them the room.

The coincidence was that the same room that they rented was prior rented b Emil Simionescu who after receiving his Ph.D. at twenty seven, he moved to Cluj University after he won the competition for a Lecturer position. His wife, the beautiful Mira, followed him, and after graduation from the engineering school, obtained an engineer position at the Clujeana Company.

Gabriel and Teodor signed the agreement for renting the apartment with engineer Popa and then invited their mother to arrange the apartment after her taste. In few days, the room looked a la carte: two beds with night stands, two desks, chairs, new rug, drapes, double wardrobe, and refrigerator in the hallway. Teodora filled up the refrigerator with everything they would need for a while; she paid the rent for ½ year in advance and left to Vaslui satisfied with what she did.

Gabriel, obtained excellent results at the Economic Sciences Institute, which he found very easy in comparison with the electro technical college; he was solicited to take a position of assistant at the new formed college. Gabriel didn't want to give up the position at the Polytechnic, but he accepted a ½ schedule for ESI. The building was opposite to the Polytechnic and superior equipped. His work load doubled, but Gabriel didn't care, he really loved it; he was testing his capacity at maximum, finding out that can do even more. The friendship with Liliana didn't make too much progress; neither of them made any proposal regarding their common future.

Alesia, her friend and roommate was preparing to move out, and Liliana started to look for a new roommate. She contacted an assistant from Mathematics, quiet, and her mind always focused on finding new solutions in the field of mathematics. From this point of view she would be a better partner for Alex, was thinking Liliana. But no, it wasn't good to make a couple from two individuals who work and think in the exact sciences fields.

The colleagues and friends didn't see Alex married so fast. During the student's years and even after, the girls were an annex preoccupation. But Alesia with her charm succeeded to produce some agitation on his latent sentiments, making him vibrate when she was around. They were, despite appearances the best pair around. He was blond, she was brunette, he engineer, she philologer; the contrasts united them.

The familiar atmosphere at the dormitories and apartments continued. The youngsters continue to meet for parties, by rotation, in various rooms. Vasile and Claudia, who married two years before wished to have a baby. Soon their dream came true. The baby, Ionuţ, has been taken by her parents to care for him; but during weekends they brought him in the building. The baby didn't feel happy to be taken from his grandparents, and cried quiet often. Other married couples, listening to Ionuţ discontent, became more careful in deciding to have a child, delaying this event.

In Iassy started the construction for building a new complex "Alexander the Good" for employees at the University. Many of the assistants signed up for being allocated one of these apartments. Gabriel asked his parents for a down payment amount, and he was one of the first on the solicitors' list. Mihai didn't want to make this commitment. He wanted to finish his doctorate and then move to Bucharest where Raluca waited for him. He already had an opening at the Fundeni's Hospital. Teodor Junior would remain alone in the apartment from Păcurari Street, renting from engineer Popa. He didn't want to follow an academic carrier. He started to work for the "The Flame of Iassy" magazine, published two volumes of poetry, was doing translations from German and English, and in his free time he painted landscapes from memory of his childhood.

In just one year a big number of the projected buildings were completed, and those on top of the list could move in. Gabriel convinced Liliana to move with him, and marry later. The following year they married in a private ceremony. Teodora could not be convinced not to give to Gabriel a real wedding party and she rented the restaurant's central hall, organizing a party to which were invited colleagues and friends and family from Vaslui and many of their collaborators from the hospital.   Gabriel was faster into getting married, but Mihai wasn't worried.   He had the doctoral thesis at which he was working intensely.   He was ready and was in the waiting period to form the examination commission: Professor Burghelea from Bucharest was one of the members, Professor Faifer and Professor Oblu both from Iassy.   Two weeks after Gabriel's wedding, Mihai received the news that the commission decided the date of September 10 for the debate of his thesis.

This was an important step in his medical career.   Ana travelled from Israel with her two children Teodor and Horace.   This was their first visit to Romania.   Raluca's parents, doctors also, wanted to participate along with their daughter to this event in Iassy. The Vancea doctors want to use this occasion to get in touch with many of their colleagues from Iassy.

The dissertation took place in the large Aula of the Medicine Institute.   Ana and other colleagues decorated the place with fresh flowers, sparing no expenses.

Mihai, clearly emotional was talking with the members of the commission waiting for the last invitees to take their seats in the hall. The meeting was opened by Professor Chipail, an eccentric figure, but with a hand of unsurpassed surgeon.   Among the young doctors was common a wish "to have a Chipail hand, and Oblu's head".   The exposure of the candidate was a total surprise, because it has been known only by his scientific conductor: A case of a heart surgery, which was supported by projected images and relevant comments. The projection device was foreign made in USA, and the surgery was performed at a hospital, a University Clinique in New York, at which Mihai assisted during his specialization.   If Mihai wouldn't have been a very well prepared candidate, maybe some of his colleagues would have accused him of immodesty.   The candidate expressed his wishes that some of these apparatus and techniques will become routine in this country as well.   The referents had only good appreciations.   The meeting ended and everyone applauded enthusiastically.   The reception hosted by Mihai's parents was an opportunity for relaxation, contentment and satisfaction.   Congratulation were addressed to Mihai as well as to his professors and especially to his parents for their efforts in raising such a great man.

The family returned to Vaslui were preparations were about to start for the marriage of Mihai and Raluca. Raluca's parents decided that they can live in their house, which was spacious enough in the Cotroceni neighborhood. They left the next day to Bucharest excited about the future groom and the beautiful family.

Ana remained in the country for a week, to re-visit the places which she didn't see since she left the country. The parents were visiting them every summer; the same did the other brothers. The two grandchildren were the joy of the whole family. Although they were for the first time in Romania, they spoke pretty well Romanian. This was Ana's decision. Horia called them daily telling them how bad he feels that he cannot join them. He cannot be away from the hospital for that long, especially away from their private Clinique.

They went to Pungeşti, and stopped at the Jewish cemetery where everyone had shed a tear. In Gârceni they didn't go, there was nobody left. Grandfather Rotaru died, and grandmother moved to Vaslui. There was just one place that needed to be visited: the canton. There was nobody living any more. The only recognizable was the old pear which was still standing. The windows and the doors of the building were covered with boards nailed. It seemed a little shorter; it was as it entered in the ground for a meter or so. The walls were in great decay. The paint started to peel from the walls remaining as an abstract mural painting. Everything looked unattended and ready to collapse at any small earth quick. In the yard only the weeds were enjoying the light through which you could see thistle gray and green lizards. From the high and solid fences remained a couple of pillars which lasted the longest being made of wood of oak.

The place looked desolate, and her feelings were those of sadness. Ana told the boys to collect acorns and pears. These things they didn't see before. Then she started to talk to the old pear tree. "What do you do my dear pear tree? Why did you have followers? Look I have two boys!" The tree moved its leaves trying to express its loneliness and sadness.

Passing through Pungeşti they tried the same sense of sadness. The Townsend was like covered in a black cloud. The war trauma, and then the new regime have put their mark over the whole town.

Those who lived there before the war were looking in vain to find a glimpse of the scattered glory everywhere over the old city.

But the star of the township Pungeşti didn't fall and maybe will send its rays of light and the town will revive getting back the old glory.

They left for Vaslui and made a stop at the Mitică Ion Inn, who rejoiced at the sight of the distinguished guests. Doctor Manea was an old acquaintance and when his family was visiting he felt much honored. The guests have been invited on the terrace in the garden, which was a private setting. The Inn was very well taken care of and it became a place for rest at the intersection of roads from Roman, Bacău, and Bârlad. The owner was a handsome man and full of money in his youth. The years of youth passed but the money were still with him. He married Natalia, who was the daughter of Manole Condrea from Porcăreţ. Natalia was twenty years younger than him, she finished the Normal School for Teachers from Vaslui, but she never made a career from teaching. She did not take care of the Inn. They hired people for those chores. Her only preoccupation was their two daughters, students at the High School in Vaslui; the parents want them to follow a medical career. They remained there for a couple of hours, trying to forget the sad impression from the visit at canton.

The time was passing as flying, and nothing could stop it. The three boys Mihai, Gabriel and Teodor left for Iassy, Ana remained with the children to spend two more days in Vaslui. There were some of her girlfriends from Lyceum who came in vacation. From the University only one of her colleagues remained medical doctor in Vaslui, she was Marieta. She was working at the Central Hospital and she was known already for her professionalism.

The hospital was the same as it was during her student's years, when Mihai and her were working with their father during their summer vacation. Perhaps she could send from Israel or other international organizations medicine or new instruments, but the regime's bureaucratic system didn't agree on any opening towards the modern world, which experienced a tremendous development after the war. Years back Horia brought some modern apparatus but the doctors could not obtain the expected results. They were not specialized or proper instructed on how accurately to handle the devices up to the performance level.

Ana and the children left by train to Bucharest where they took a flight to Tel Aviv. Raluca waited for her at the train station and then took her to the airport. Ana promised that she'll return to Romania at their wedding.

*

The confirmation of Mihai as doctor in medical sciences came quiet fast, in just few weeks.

That fall he had two invitations to some international conferences; one at Moscow, where he never been, and the other to America. There were circulated a lot of rumors about the Russian security. But the Russians had a good school of medicine with which Mihai wanted to make contact. Otherwise he needed to be prudent. His invitation to Moscow came from two colleagues whom he met at a congress in New York and with whom he kept in contact. Taking into account their names and their relations with the Americans, it seemed that they were Jews. During High School Mihai studied Russian, but he neglected to practice. Now, he wanted that in two month he wanted to remember everything and also to add the medical terminology. He was convinced that he'll be able to communicate if not in Russian, in English for sure.

Certainly, the Russians realized that most international conferences were in English and they wanted to continue on this path. He prepared his communication in English but attached a Russian abstract. Raluca didn't go with Mihai because the Russians didn't invite her, but they were scheduled to go together at the next conference which would be held in America, and where his uncle Flavius was interested to meet her.

He refreshed his knowledge of Russian and he was thinking that it was good that his parents asked him to pay attention to all school subjects, and that included Russian language. In two months reading and listening to tapes he was able to handle a light conversation.

Moscow is a city apart, surprisingly beautiful. The GUM, which is a big store, can take all your money if you are not selective. The Kremlin, with its streets in a semicircle, is of a special beauty. The Red Square's name doesn't have anything in common with the red army, hosts some unique cultural monuments: Cathedral "St. Basil", Bolshoi Theatre (one of the world renown), Lenin's mausoleum. The golden towers century-old create an atmosphere from the Russian legends, which can be found only in Moscow. A permanent flame is guarding the Russian hero's monument along with the Russian guards. The tower and the bell, the largest in the world, unfortunately with the needle and the tune solidified give height and majesty to the entire landscape.

The Kremlin which clustered around many of its monuments and churches on the sunny days was reflecting the light of the golden towers of the old buildings around

The congress from Moscow went on as any international congress. The Russians knew that is the nation's prestige to be prepared in showing to the participants the highest professionalism. They were taken to Leningrad (Petersburg) the Old Russian capital, to the Winter Palace, the Hermitage museum, which seriously competes with Louvre.

Mihai was shocked by the subway in Moscow. It is an architectural marvel. The stations were hosting true art operas. About the metro Mihai was told a fanny legend. The metro architects and constructors presented to Stalin their planes. While studying the plans, Stalin placed his tea cup on them. The trace left by the cup on the map has been interpreted by the architects the route that should be followed, and the more visible spots were interpreted as the stations which have turned into really small museums with columns, mural paintings and sculptures done by Russian artists. Mihai had never seen anything like this in any of the metros in the world. He returned home excited not only by the medical knowledge but also by the artistic values of the Russian culture.

Relaxed he resumed his work at the hospital. At his age of twenty eight his medical knowledge were impressive, but he didn't have the courage to perform a difficult surgery. His interventions were performed only when he was in the emergency room. His know how, and all details have not been explored yet remaining in the shadow of his professor Chipail. One day the professor gave him the surgical knife and took the second place. It was a stomach complicated intervention. "Mihai, I don't feel good today, my hands are shaking, please perform this operation, I will assist you, and I will intervene if necessary." The young doctor took his role seriously, making the first incision straight as drawn along a ruler. The operation followed a normal path. The assistant wiped the drops of ice-cold sweat from his forehead. While working he was asking the anesthesiologist, just by looking at him, about the blood pressure and all vital signs of the patient. An artistic closing of the cut concluded the surgery.   He followed the patient until he was convinced that everything regarding his vital functions was on a normal path.

He overcame the biggest obstacle of his chirurgical career. But from here until the time when any intervention would become normal for a chirurgical doctor there was a long way.   The calm, balanced, self-control, timeless, safeties are sine qua non qualities and conditions for a surgeon. The professor followed all his reactions and his precision during the operation from the way he handled the knife until the beads of sweat, a sign of total concentration. In the office the professor congratulated him and praised him in an original way; "Dear Mihai, now you can call me "you"." When he arrived home he called Raluca immediately, telling her about his performance that day when was daunting at first but he was called to be number one hand and Chipail was hand number 2.   His accumulated theoretical knowledge became now successfully applied in practice.   But the science gets updated continuously, and only keeping up, and practicing the new techniques one can become efficient and precise. It is like in mathematics; a plus or a minus inversed would produce a different result and sometimes a serious error.

Now, Mihai was performing operations not only during his emergency hours, but any time when he was asked to.   He was following the patients' recovery until they were released from the hospital. The best anesthesiologist in the hospital was a lady about forty years, she was the head of the section, Mrs. Georgiana Manolescu. Often Mrs. Manolescu was worth more than a surgeon. Before surgery she made a complex clinical picture of the patient in detail.   During the intervention, she was focused not only on the patient but also to the surgeon being ready for any emergency situations dictated by the doctor. With a remarkable professionalism she followed the patient to the intensive care and after. One time, when Mihai was at the University, teaching, one of his patients became ill. Mrs. Manolescu ordered a perfusion to the patient with medication from her section gesture very much appreciated by Mihai who went to personally thank her. She was in her break reading. During their discussion, Mihai found out that Mrs. Manolescu liked very much to read; this explained one of her qualities, great sensitivity.   Unfortunately, not all anesthesiologists were equally conscious, in regards to the big responsibility for each patient, leaving a lot of tasks to the surgeon.

During the month of November took place the American Congress at which professor Oblu was also invited. Mihai translated his presentation papers in English. The professor spoke only German and French. English wasn't the selected language when he was younger. While preparing for Congress, the professor invited Mihai at his residence to discuss both their presentations. He lived alone. Hiss residence was a true museum. The walls were upholstered with valuable paintings of Grigorescu, Aman, Luchian, Agafitei, and Hatman, all renown painters. The professor liked to discuss with the young doctors, probably he was searching for a disciple. Most of his life he was pursued by misfortune. His only daughter, assistant, colleague with Gabriel, in a hot day, while walking on the street had a serious stroke. People, in rush, passed by and didn't pay much attention to her. She was transported to the hospital, but it was too late. She entered in a comma. Colleagues from abroad sent all the possible medicine. The professor who saved so many lives, remained incapable to save is daughter. After months of coma, her daughter's live ended. The professor hardly recovered, continuing with the same commitment to serve his profession.

The Congress to which he'll participate with Mihai excited him. He had never been in the U.S. and was happy to have Mihai with him.

Mihai left for Bucharest one day earlier. The plane from Iassy to Bucharest which professor Oblu took crashed due to technicalities near Bacau. All passengers died with the exception of a baby who was on his mother lap. The Romanian medicine was shaken by the loss of a great professor.

Next day Raluca and Mihai left for New York, the flight was a continuous stress, both of them being deeply touched by the airplane accident. The congress began its work keeping a moment of silence in the memory of the Romanian professor.

Uncle Flavius, as usual, waited for his nephew at the airport and brought them to his home. He liked Raluca from the first moment. Uncle Flavius became kind of earthly demiurge who knew everything, and arranging things, as he thought is best. He didn't succeed to take Mihai under his direct protection, but probably, he paid good money for Ana. Underground talk was that all Jews who left sent to the Romanian state a considerable amount of money, deposited in as secret special secret account. Ana's departure happened very quickly, and then all parents' visits every year in Israel, while others couldn't travel even to Yugoslavia, was a mystery which couldn't be understood easily. He knew more about Raluca than Mihai. His friends from Bucharest informed him immediately after their marriage, about all her biographical data. Her grandparents from mother's part, before the war were owners of a chain of stores in Dudesti. Veronica, their daughter married during college her colleague David Vancea. The parents had the inspiration to buy a house in Cotroceni for the young doctors. They had their own aspirations. They didn't want to have Veronica live in a merchant environment but in an upper class neighborhood. The rebellion from 1941 and the bombardments which occurred totally destroyed the Dudesti neighborhood, and the old merchants remained almost depleted, but escaped with their lives. The Decree from 1945 about the nationalization they succeeded to maintain only one building which remained upright. The business didn't go for long because of the new regime, but the elders were holding well because of their money saved for a rainy day. They were glad that their daughter and son in law worked at the largest hospital in Bucharest.

All of these details have been provided to the old doctor by his friends, and was very happy that Raluca was one of theirs. He didn't want to tell to Mihai any of these details. In fact Mihai was raised in a loving family as in a nest of precious swallows, to which adding his profession was certain that any bias was null and would not affect him in any way.

To the young couple as well as other nephews who came to various congresses, he offered a car and a driver. The participants at the congress seeing their impeccable attire, their professional achievements, thought that Romania is the country of honey and milk.

Flavius Solomon asked Raluca to call him, just uncle Flavius, as Mihai did. Raluca accepted with great pleasure, considering this as a sign of integration in the family.

The sojourn in New York was beneficial to the two from professional and spiritual point of view. Mihai received, at his request, a projector, which he intended to use it during his lectures back home at the University. Another valuable gift was a powerful microscope, which was indispensable to a surgeon, it looked as jewelry; he couldn't ask for more from his uncle. Raluca had already one of these instruments as powerful as this. A good surgeon cannot do plastic surgery, as he wanted without such an instrument.

In Bucharest, at the Fundeni's Hospital where Raluca finished her internship, she remained involved in this new branch of plastic surgery, working with Doctor Agrippa Ionescu, the founder of the Romanian school of plastic surgery.

It was December. The Fundeni hospital's management has approved the transfer of Doctor Mihai Manea from the Parhon Hospital to the Fundeni Hospital. The doctor had to take his new position starting January 1. The arrangements were that he will live at Raluca's parents. At this time Raluca and Mihai decided to legalize their marriage very soon. The civil ceremony took place in Bucharest, without a special fest.

As a physician, Mihai, preferred the emergency hospital where he could acquire a lot of experience, but he was thankful for the position he received. At this hospital were working many renown doctors in the Romania medicine, and therefore, he would be exposed to a lot of learning.

His professor, in the first day, gave him the surgeon knife counting on his knowledge and experience from the Iassy school.

His father in law, Doctor David Vancea stayed in the shadow, and followed the results of his son in law, acquired through his own hard work. Mihai didn't disappoint anyone. At most of the conferences he participated abroad, he received invitations to relocate in those centers. The invitations came from U.S.A., Italy, Belgium, but he didn't want to leave his country.

Mihai had the feeling that his visits out of the country will be limited from now on after he moved to Bucharest. But, just then he received an invitation for which he waited for a long while. It was an invitation to a Chirurgical Congress in China. He met some Chinese and Japanese colleagues at various congresses, but his impression was that they were not too receptive to the European achievements. China was a country that surprised for him from all points of view. Their innate patriotism wasn't just a show off, but a profound sense of love to parents, modesty, diligence and tenacity of sustainability, and civilization designed for eternity.

The university clinic in Beijing performed for foreign guests two operations under anesthesia based on acupuncture. The guests were stunned when the patient, who had a brain surgery sat up on the operating table, waving to the guests after the needles have been pulled out. Was that reality or trick? It was reality.

The foreign doctors were shown several places around the city as traditionally is done during such conferences; The Chinese wall, the biggest construction on Earth, which can be seen from the Moon, the famous cultivated terraces, the imperial palaces, the metro, the underground city and many other places. The visitors remained very impressed by the achievements of an old country and the civilization which will never pass in anonymity.

Mihai returned home with a plus in his knowledge about a nation with traditions which cannot be, sometimes, understood, if you don't integrate a little in its historic spirituality, geography and existence. It took a long time to tell Raluca everything about the unseen face of China, and they decided that with next occasion they'll go together to visit the grate country from the Far East. He was so excited that he needed to talk about his experience to his parents. And next Saturday they left by train to Vaslui, informing his brothers from Iassy also. It was a great day.

Gabriel and Liliana, married for a couple of years were waiting for a baby – Liliana just finished her doctorate, becoming also an assistant professor.

Teodor Junior was still preoccupied with books, poetry, literary Iassy, theatre, philharmonic, expositions and many other cultural events. There were no signs of any connection from sentimental point of view. He didn't have any girlfriends and none interested him. On campus, in the building for young people without family, every year arrived girls that were smart and beautiful. Gabriel and Liliana could introduce him to them, but Teodor didn't manifest any erotic desire. He was living in the same place with the engineer Popa who reached an honorable age and was still single.

The visit to Vaslui of all the children was short, as a zephyr of spring, but the parents were satisfied and thanked to all of them for coming.

The Easter Holiday for those in Bucharest passed unobserved. Mihai and Raluca had to work a lot in the emergency rooms. Their professors, high in seniority, could take time off during holidays, having the young doctors to work the holidays. Just one festive lunch in the Easter day, that was the only time for to relax.

Mihai was thinking at those holidays back home when he was a child, with the smell of backed panetone, carefully painted eggs done by Vasilica. All of these images looked now, when he became mature, dreams from childhood.

We all keep coming back to the past, which is the longest. The present which is very short, and about the future, what can be said? It is uncertain and unsure.

The month of May, the most beautiful, came with dramatic news for some.

One night, long after mid night, Mihai was awakened by an international phone call from U.S.A. He thought that it is about an international congress and because of the time zone, there was day time. It wasn't so. On the phone, a deep voice at the other end announced that Doctor Flavius Solomon died. In an hour the phone rang again, this time from Tel Aviv, and a woman's voice crying announced the same news. It was Ana. She and Horia flew immediately to New York.

Mihai couldn't leave. He needed visa and then a plane ticket. Ana knew the laws of the country, so she advised him to stay calm because the relatives know the situation from Romania. Mihai asked Ana to come, when she can, to tell them more details about uncle Flavius. In a week Ana returned to Bucharest directly from New York and together went to Vaslui. The children remained in Israel, Horace being in school, first grade.

Ana brought with her many copies from the wills and Flavius Solomon's properties. The Doctor died due to a cardio-respiratory arrest. The cleaning woman Varina, who lived in the house and the wife of his driver Osei, found him dead in his armchair in front of the TV which was on. He had the easiest death. He didn't think at his age of his deficiencies, neither at those who he loved, and were left in pain.

At the funeral people gathered from all over the world, relatives or friends from Israel, Switzerland, England. Ana saw most of them for the first time, but they appeared as they knew each other for a long time. Maybe uncle Flavius told them about Ana and Mihai. Many asked about Mihai, why he didn't come. Ana excused him telling them that from Romania one cannot leave whenever he wants, even to a funeral.

There were cases when musicians or scientists who needed to travel for important meetings or contracts, received the visa long after the event took place or the contract expired. There was a fable that was going around, which probably had some truth. A head of an ethnic group from Craiova was invited to a meeting of their ethnicity somewhere in Europe. He submitted the paperwork for visa well in advance. His visa approval came after a month, after the closing of their congress. The man called the Passport Services and told to the officer that he thanks him but he already went Berlin at the conference and now he's back. The officer remained perplex but he could not believe that such a thing was possible.

After funeral, Doctor Flavius Solomon's lawyer opened and read the will in a meeting with all relatives. To each relative he left something. The most favored were the three nephews: Horia, Mihai and Ana. The house in New York was left to all three of them with the condition that Varina and Osei will live there as long as they want, receiving payment for maintenance. The house from Florida was left to a niece of second grade with three children..

All his other properties (home, medical cabinet, stocks) were left to Horia and Ana. Ana's name was always mentioned alongside with Horia, and again Ana had doubts in relation to his secrets which will continue to remain secrets. For Mihai remained the home from Geneva, provided it will never be sold; this was another secret. To each of the three was listed one million dollars, which were in a bank in Switzerland, one million should be donated to orphanages, as they will decide. The David's start, the Solomon family was inherited by Horia Solomon.

Manea's family remained overwhelmed in front of the disclosure of the will documentation. The communist Romania, the laws regarding the foreign accounts, and in particular foreign currency were very strict. Uncle Flavius knew all of these and that was the reason for leaving the money in Suisse bank.

In Switzerland, the house was half rented for a period of five years. The contract stipulated that they had to provide maintenance to the whole property. Regarding the money in dollars, Ana told the family, that the accounts shouldn't be touched. The bank had the obligation to maintain the secrecy of the amount and their owners. At the moment the accounts were on Flavius Solomon's name. When necessary, Mihai could use the will. The most important thing was that this secret should be carefully kept. Ana and Mihai left to Bucharest. Mihai didn't know how to proceed with Raluca, with which he didn't have any secrets. It was decide, however, not to say anything since his wife's name didn't appear on any accounts and any property. Ana went to Tel Aviv and told Horia that her twin gave her the liberty and empowerment to deal with his part of the will. Ana somehow had a small worry. "What if one day the security will find out something about the will?" He will negate everything, saying that he renounced everything in his sister's favor. The Romanian security wasn't too advanced as that form America or Russia, and so his worried shouldn't even exist.

A few days after the death of his uncle Flavius, Mihai was invited to the office of Professor Proca. The professor was Deputy Prime Minister and government advisor. He wasn't honored by these functions, ad he didn't ask for them, but was forced to accept. In all social and political organizations was necessary to include personalities with moral and professional authority. Any refusal of a function entails harm and abuse that could damage his profession.

Professor Proca didn't quit his position at Fundeni Hospital. He retains his office, performing operations requested by patients. Among his colleagues and collaborators his attitude was the same, only that sometimes he had to intervene in their favor, especially when he was asked for help in obtaining visa to travel abroad. "Please sit down Mihai" said the Professor. "Please accept my condolences for the death of your uncle. We were colleagues at the University and I felt the burden of the injustice committed against the Jewish fathers. After he escaped from Transnistria and went to America, we met; he asked me to look after you from the distance, but you are so good, that you don't need anyone's protection. Regarding your application for the position of Professor, what is the status?" "Thank you for everything Professor, I hope that my application will be approved."

Mihai raised, thanked to the Professor one more time and left. Walking the hospital hallways Mihai was thinking at how small the world is. He would have stayed longer in the Professor's office but he was afraid of other questions. Mihai couldn't assume what Professor Proca knows about him, and he preferred to conclude the conversation. Perhaps, he reflected, the Professor knows simply that he is his nephew and no other details.

Two weeks later came also the decision that Mihai Manea, doctor in medical sciences, received the title of associate professor following the selection of the applications for the this position. The students appreciated him. In the hospital the operations were scheduled one after the other. He was solicited to teach also at the University Hospital. At Iassy, his professor was calling for him for a special operation. The older professors were living frustrating times. They have not been exposed to the English language in their time, as the young generation. Some struggled to learn it and were now more relaxed. Mihai and Raluca were solicited to translate their communications in English.

Mihai and Raluca's desire was to go to India and Japan; these being different cultures with different cultural traditions. After their twins were born, Raluca had to stop for a while her travelling plans. Not all things can be planned always in advanced. When their twins were two month old, Mihai had a chance to go to Japan to a congress, so he had to go alone this time. He returned with the same enthusiasm as he returned from China. In Tokyo he caught a substantial earthquake, but the Japanese were used with these movements of the earth and didn't pay too much attention. Mihai was very captivated by the new knowledge.

After two months of leave Raluca returned to work with Professor Agripa Ionescu. She started to get very good in reconstructions and modelling of facial characteristics, giving to the patient the desired result.

Gabriel started to travel also. His preoccupations lately were on the economic side. He obtained from the Institute of Economic Sciences a position of professor. He had classes also at the Polytechnic. He competed with a colleague for a promotion but she has been selected because she had two children. This selection criterion was the standard on those days. The social-politic criteria were valued more than the professional qualities.

In a couple of weeks to Manea's family was added another member; the lovely Maria, Gabriel's daughter. After four grandsons, now the darling Maria was the new star in the family. Grandma Teodora took time off and moved temporarily to Iassy. For Gabriel, Teodora always had a special feeling. Inside she still could not forget the fact that she had to change his father's name Simionescu, although this was done for his own interest. Liliana's both parents passed during a car accident when she was still in High School. Helped by relatives she continued her studies and obtained a scholarship. She finished her studies, and now God gave her a daughter. Teodora became a mother to her.

Gabriel didn't find out any secrets of Manea's family, which from his point of view was a perfect family. Teodora installed herself in Iassy taking seriously her grandmother duties, while Liliana went to school.

In Bucharest the Institute of Economic Sciences was preparing an International seminar at which Gabriel was invited to present a communication. His colleagues knew that he combined the electrical engineering and economic sciences obtaining noticeable results. When he selected his topic he consulted also with Professor N.N Constantinescu (who wasn't academician yet). The Institute of Economic Sciences from Iassy was new, there were not international renowned professors. The communication presented by Gabriel Manea (in Romanian and English) was received with great interest and Professor Mehedințu and Niță Dobrotă tried to test the ground and find out what are Gabriel's intensions and proposing to him a position at their Institute. Gabriel didn't refuse, demanding, however some time to reflect.

In the meantime, Ana who was following the International conferences at the University of Tel Aviv enrolled Gabriel with a communication for the month of July, and sent him the invitation and the agenda with various attachments. All have been sent officially at Iassy. The rector from Iassy received a letter that stated that the invitation is the result of his valuable conference in Bucharest. The approvals for Manea's family weren't a problem. Every time they received the approvals and they always returned home. Gabriel travel to Belgrade and Vienna without Liliana.

Teodor Junior travelled with the writers and journalists several times. Last time he travelled with a delegation of the party to London. He had a special talent for foreign languages. He spoke fluently French, English, German, Russian, and recently he started to learn Arabic with some friends who studied in Romania.

For the Tell-Aviv conference, Gabriel choose a topic with an introduction in the Gabriel has chosen to Tel Aviv an exciting topic with an introduction into the world capitalist economy and with reference to the socialist economy without denying the principles neither of capitalist economic development nor to exaggerate the benefits of socialist economy. More than the introduction, he prepared a series of data and other information to be able to answer the questions with examples in regards to the socialist economy. Horia waited for him at the airport. Horia preferred to stay at the hotel with other participants from other countries. He stayed two extra days. He learned everything he could find in the free world, establishing and making friends and promising to meet and participate in the next meeting in Belgium. He regretted that Liliana is not with him, but in life there are sacrifices, as that of a mother.

The days spent in Israel after the conference gave him another perspective about those places. Jerusalem appeared to be as the one from history and legends from fifteen century Before Christ. A city with a turbulent history, occupied by Babylonians, Egyptians, Syrians, Romans, Turks, and it resisted miraculously to all these times. The Citi of David, King Solomon's temple, The Wailing Wall, The Church of the Holy Grave, The Hebrew University and many other artifacts are testimonies of an imperishable past. In Tel-Aviv, besides the University, Gabriel visited museums, old and new buildings, properly maintained. He talked a lot about Maria and Ana's children were curious to know how their cousin looks like. He showed them a small photo, where Maria appeared as a little princess.

Ana prepared another surprise for Gabriel. She made arrangements that he'll meet Tina, who was living in Tel-Aviv. Ana met her on the street exactly the year she moved to Israel. From there on they kept in touch by phone, talking about the years, when they all were students. When she was sure that Gabriel will come to Israel Ana got in touch with Tina and made arrangements to get together with Gabriel. The three of them met for coffee and talked about the years spent together on campus in Iassy. They were now more mature, but unchanged. The time was good with their appearance. Ana was very happy, which was reflected on her beautiful still childish face. Tina with her big, blue eyes had the same blond and curly hair. Gabriel was the same retained and sturdy in gestures. They talked about the situation in the country, but mostly about their professors, the about their common friends who went all over the great Earth finding new places to live and work.

Manea's family was doing well in Romania and the fact the Ana left the country did not get those who remained behind any trouble.   Actually, her presence outside the country was as an angel who makes sure that all of them are well. She was helping them from far away just through her existence.

The visit in Israel gave to Gabriel a plus of energy, re-charged him. He found some friends with whom he exchanged business cards, and promised each other to meet again at other seminars or conferences.

At return he remained an extra day in Bucharest at Mihai's residence. He got the impression that the scientific life in Bucharest is superior to that from Iassy, and noticed that Mihai was suggesting moving to Bucharest. This idea pleased him.

Back home in Iassy, Liliana, little Maria and Teodora worried for him. The questions about Ana and her family were pouring from Teodora. Gabriel was talking continuously about everything walking around with little Maria in his arms. He didn't see her for a week, and he noticed that she is bigger now, and more beautiful.

In the evening when Maria was sleeping, Gabriel told Liliana about his intensions to move to Bucharest. Liliana didn't oppose. In their family the big decisions were on Gabriel's shoulders.

*

The villa from Doctor Lister Street was completely renovated and now the owners were moving in. The mansion had separate apartments, one for Mihai and the other for Gabriel. Both apartments had basement, ground floor, and two floors. Above there was a spacious attic. There was also a large balcony of white marble with nice decorations. Nice lateral stairs with handrail which stopped in front of two massive doors with crystal and steel ornaments.

Each apartment had a separate entrance. The house was old and no one knew who the owners were many decades ago. Only a small inscription mentioned the architect's name Aurel Crețu. The last owner left the country and sold the house at a modest price. Raluca and Mihai Manea were the first to move in from Raluca's parents. Gabriel's apartment remained empty for several months because at Iassy Gabriel had to close some business at the University and Liliana was scheduled to start working at the Chemistry Institute whose patron was Elena Ceausescu. Gabriel received his transfer papers for a position at the Institute of Economic Sciences at the External Commerce. The little Maria was left at Vaslui under the care of Teodora and Vasilica. Everyone suggested to Liliana to have another baby, but she wanted first to finish her doctorate. Her decision was very wise, because this was an essential condition to obtain the position in Bucharest.

The house was bought with the money sent by Ana from the bank account left by uncle Flavius. At that time in the country many things were very strict, and Ana and Horia kept the communication through the lawyer who represented the whole family.

Mihai was still hesitant to confess to Raluca about the inheritance from uncle Flavius. He hoped that such a day will come sometime in the future. They wanted, that together they could travel somewhere to a conference in Switzerland and then he'll surprise her. After many months of waiting the news of such a conference came, and Mihai received an invitation. He called Ana to do something, such that Raluca will get a visa without special invitation, and to travel as participant on her expenses. It was a great surprise when Raluca received the approval to travel with Mihai to Switzerland. He was very curious to see his house left to him by uncle Flavius.

It was his first visit to Geneva. At the airport two organizers waited for them. They spoke French, German and English, but the greatest surprise was Ana, who took some time off to meet Mihai. Ana was familiar with the house, and the people who lived there. Mihai has been introduced as the owner. Ana took care to extend their contract for other five years. Raluca was very surprised. She didn't know anything about the house, and bank accounts. But she understood why Mihai couldn't tell her anything. Mihai continued to ask Ana to have everything taken care of through the lawyer since in Romania these types of transactions could be disastrous for the whole family. In Romania was impossible to have properties or bank accounts in foreign countries. All the original documents were with Ana and a set of copies with his parents in Vaslui.

Ana gave them the money she received from rent and Raluca, now had some pocket money for shopping.

The property was a two floor large house, with the interior recently updated, the furniture was old but well maintained. The garage and other small rooms underground had a special entry. The laundry room was like a saloon. The library room and music room at the first floor, also at the first floor were the dining room and the kitchen. The bedrooms each with their bathroom were at the second floor. Also at the second floor was the children's play room. More rooms were arranged for guests. In a country such as Switzerland with 25 cantons – one can benefit of such a home. The two people who were living there were two Jews of Polish origin. They were the only ones who survived the war atrocities directed towards the Jewish people. Doctor Solomon knew them well and often they talked about his grandchildren from Romania; when they met them, it seemed that they knew them for long, long time. The house was prepared for the guest owners. They spent an evening in family. The merchant had a small shop of dairy products, and offered to his guests products from his store.

Ana, Raluca and Mihai participated at the conference interested to find out what was new in medicine in the rest of the world. Ana came just to see his brother, to show him the house, to relax for a couple of days, but she couldn't refrain nor to participate at the conference. She met with other colleagues from other countries and she found it very pleasant.

Mihai's communication in the plena of the conference was very interesting for those from Switzerland, and he received a verbal invitation for the following conference in relation to the activity of the International Organization of Health with the headquarters in Geneva.

Ana left first. Next summer she was waiting for Mihai and Raluca in Israel during their vacation. Mihai was familiar with Ana's adoptive country, but Raluca didn't visit it yet.

Raluca and Mihai without comments thought the same thing they were trying to make a comparison between Romania and Switzerland, but could not find any reference points. What was that kept Mihai connected to Romania? It was an unseen root which was feeding him with a sweet sap from the ancestral lands. If this root dries out, as it happens many times in life, then they can go any place in the world.

Mihai had an undisclosed issue, many times he was feeling, how Teodora was thinking as he had two souls. When he was going to the grave of his relatives, where the other Mihai was buried, a strange sentiment was taking over his thinking and was tented to talk in his head "What do you do, my dear?" was asking Mihai Manea, and the other Mihai, as child was appearing for a fraction of a second smiling.

Since they moved to Bucharest, they went less often to Vaslui; the parents disappointed in a way understood the circumstances. Every time they went to Vaslui, they paid their visit to Pungeşti at the graves of their relatives.

During the summer Liliana and Gabriel moved in their new apartment on Doctor Lister Street. At beginning they felt very uncomfortable finding that Ana paid all, but the parents said that they shouldn't worry because they also contributed to the payment. Another secret surfaced. The apartment from Iassy remained to Teodor who didn't rush to move in. He was a bohemian type of artist without any interest for the practical aspect of life wasn't as any of his siblings.

Teodora and Teodor Manea took advantage of some vacation and went to Bucharest to help the children move in the new house. Raluca had some help from her parents, but Liliana's parents became Teodora and Teodor Manea. Teodora's special attachment for Gabriel was observed by everyone. No one displayed any jealous sentiments. They called him "mommy's curly", due to his black and curly hair.

The approval for Gabriel's transfer came as expected and his starting date should have been September 1, at the institute of Exterior Commerce. For Liliana the papers for transfer took longer. The security was conducting a serious investigation for her appointment at the Chemistry Institute. There were no problems to worry about. She didn't have parents and other siblings, or relatives who escaped out of the country. Gabriel became member of the Communist party, as well as the rest of the family. It was known that Ana left the country legally through marriage, and probably being paid big money for her. The relations between Israel and Romania were good.

The month of September was approaching but Liliana didn't receive the approval for the engineer chemist. Only with two days before September 1 she received the approval. The Dean from the Iassy Chemistry Department was disappointed that his best project leader from the Chemistry Laboratory is leaving, but he understood that her family is above everything.

The house from Bucharest seemed too big for Liliana, but she remembered that no one should complain about too much luck. The only disadvantage was that the house didn't have a larger garden. Maria who grew up in Vaslui was spoiled in the grandparents' garden and she was missing playing outside. During the school season she was dreaming to come back in vacation at her grandparents. Also in the summer her cousins from Israel were coming to spend some time with the grandparents. They were always very nice to their cousin Maria and they looked after her like after a sister.

The day of September 1, when Liliana and Gabriel went to work in Bucharest they had to open new doors, it was, for both of them, a new beginning. Gabriel was pretty much known by his new colleagues, but Liliana was stepping in a large Institution where she would have other problems and responsibilities.

The lead engineer, a very nice lady, met her warmly, introducing her to the overall formalities of the place and specifically to her section. Listening to her Liliana had the impression that she is a high class engineer. She was introduced to various offices and presented to other employees with who she'll collaborate. Liliana was dressed simple but elegant, her hair was also combed carefully, and makeup was very discrete. In the beginning the colleagues were reserved because of her credentials of doctor in chemistry and her activity at the University. In time, however, they became convinced that she was one of them.

The first advice she received from her colleagues was to pay special attention to what she talks because in this institution out of ten people one of them is from Security. They told her that when Mrs. Comes in visit, or for a meeting to stay away from her, and do not wear makeup or any other things that would attract her attention. Her boss being a beautiful lady, never sit in the first row in the meetings, because the first Lady of the country was allergic to beautiful and smart ladies. This is what happened to the wife of the Ambassador Corneliu Manescu, Dana or with Violeta Andrei. She could not agree to be seen in the same spot with other women who were nicer looking than her. Ones, the Ceausescu family was in a protocol visit to a tropical Asiatic country. The protocol was that the wife of the Ambassador will accompany the First Lady. The wife of the Ambassador went to the guest house were Elena and Nicolae Ceausescu were hosted. Looking through the windows, the First Lady sees a very elegant and beautiful lady, with a nice white hat. When she was told that this was the wife of the Ambassador, she made a nervous crisis, asking that the wife is not needed because she doesn't need a companion. She decided to travel in that trip alone with just the translator. In a month afterwards, the Ambassador has been recalled and didn't get any other assignment.

*

December 1989. Every corner of the world has its own holiday. Holidays, in general are sources of joy, occasions for happiness, humility, forgiveness, and celebration. In many households the efforts for preparations in the eve of holidays is excessive, ambitious, expensive and fatiguing. For these who exceed in their preparations for celebrating Christmas, Romanians have a proverb "Christmas doesn't come with a bat." This Christmas for Romanians came with a bat, and even more than that.

To pay all debts of the country, as a result of excessive borrowing or impositions of other countries, the head of the party had to tighten the belt. This ambition has crossed the line, and the country's tolerance reached its margins. People could not find anything for food in the state owned stores. People were staying in line for hours to buy a pack of butter or some skinny chickens. Al reports regarding the industrial and agricultural productions were inflated, and exaggerated. The lie had very long legs, but the most loved son of the Romanian people was faking that he doesn't know that something could be wrong. There was a joke, actually very sad reality. At a pig farm, a pig gave birth to eight piglets. The farm's boss reported that there were 12 piglets, and from an exaggeration to the other, the last number reported was 16 piglets. The general secretary decided that eight piglets should be exported and the rest eight to be used for internal consumption. This type of grossly inflated reporting lead to the lack of produce for the internal consumption. Therefore, the population was hungry and rose to a general revolt bursting the belt over tightened.

On Christmas Eve, with the first snowflakes, paradoxically, the revolt spirit of the people sparked. People died, innocent blood poured, but there the first seeds of democracy have been sawn. The hopes soared. All thought that the victory is on the side of suffering people.

The Iron Curtains fell, the solid walls, have been destroyed, the communist governments have crumbled, and the world was going ahead, each, and everyone how they could.

Mihai remained days and nights on end in the hospital. He received the news about the revolution through the blood of the wounded.

Gabriel spent a day and a night with his students at the Television station, and then he withdrew because the future of how the country will be handled was decided.

The Christmas was celebrated with guns and bullets, and in a simulated trial the Ceausescu has been charged and condemned to death. The execution took place in the courtyard of the barracks in Targoviste.

It followed the struggle for power, the privatization was done in secret commissions; the frauds from the state property could not be controlled; many got rich over nigh.

The streets were patrolled by soldiers and the tanks on the streets ready to attack. The old generals didn't distribute their roles and the orders were contradictory. The people in the street who gathered in the first hours of the revolution or joined the next day the revolutionaries sensing that there is something to take advantage by being on those premises, and put their names and addresses on various lists of participation in various revolutionary activities, such as defending the TV station, the radio station, the University, and other important sites. For the true revolutionaries who died, or have been wounded people have their respect and consideration, but those who falsely portrait as revolutionaries should be eliminated and ashamed of their dishonesties. Gabriel had a colleague who lived on one of the streets near the TV station, and he probably came out into the street to see what happens. He became, later on, a revolutionary, along with his whole family, receiving certificates of outstanding revolutionary. Some received not only simple certificates, they received house and land compensation and monetary payments which were as much as a University Professor salary for one year. Asking some of his colleague what did they do, and what were their merits. He answer nonchalantly that he brought coffee and tea to the soldiers and the guardians at the TV station.

Gabriel, who stood on the barricades twenty-four hours with his students, did not ask for certificates. What he did was his conscience dictated to him as Romanian. Later, as economist, he'll argue that it is a national crime to sell everything to some foreigners, inclusive the Dacian gold. But, what about those who received the commission? Perhaps the voice of the Romanian Academy will be heard.

In the fall of 1990 dozens of private Universities invited the High School absolvents who fail to enter to the traditional state University to become their students. Thousands of young absolvents who "didn't want to miss the train" enrolled for a considerable tax, with exams or special tests.   Most Universities of this type were opened in Bucharest with sites available in other cities of the country. The classes were offered during the day or in the evening; some were without attendance for those who didn't live in these centers.

To attract many students, the universities hired prestigious professors who were better paid than at the state Universities.

After revolution, Gabriel revisited his folder application for the professor position, which was pushed aside by the University for the last couple of years. He hoped that after the revolution his real scientific and teaching qualities will prevail. And, indeed he was right. At the beginning of the University year he became Professor. He couldn't answer any more to the solicitations of a full time position for the private Universities. He maintained a few hours at a private University. He was looking for an increase in the quality of the taught material. He knew that abroad the private universities are among the best in the world.

After a year of teaching at the privates, he made already his own opinion about the scientific level of the University. He kept his opinions for himself. The majority of students were from families who started to make fast money. There were also students from modest families who didn't have money for private preparations and were coming from industrial lyceums. For these students, Gabriel developed a sentiment of compassion. He wanted to suggest that these new formed Universities should give some scholarships or reduced taxes. He lost, in his mind only, because he noticed that the raise for the money was a tough one. At the beginning before starting his lectures, Professor Gabriel Manea introduced himself to the Dean with a handful of international projects for which he suggested that their University can enroll. He engaged to be the coordinator of one of these projects with the condition that he'll be provided with a small room where he can conduct the project. That day he was assigned the room with desks and chairs. Helped by the assistant Codrin he bought two computers for the new laboratory. For a lecture room he provided several computers for students which were sponsored by some banks. Assistant Codrin started to work with the students.

When the new semester started they found out that two of the students who participated at the project didn't enroll any more due to lack of money. Interestingly enough, the number of the freshmen increased. It was like a roller coaster. The students flooded for the first semester, but didn't show up for the second semester due to high taxes.

On several occasions Codrin expressed his outrage against the University, which charges too high fees. Professor Manea tried to calm him down, thinking that shortly things will be arranged. He made a habit from offering to secretaries and clerks small gifts; coffee for example. The clerks, who were inundated with paper work for students' admission, appreciated his gestures and gave priority to his students; he also found that the drawers were full of cash and applications. It was suppose that the cash should be deposited to the bank after they would divide the money among themselves, the rector taking the largest amount. The Professor didn't give too much attention to Codrin's disclosure but he knew what it has to be done. He went home. The dinner wasn't ready yet, and he went to see his brother Mihai.

Checked out the alarm system installed with the help of his assistant. At that time he discovered his assistant's aptitude for electronics. He was surprised to find out that Codrin had the same hobby as is: cryptography and encryption. The coincidence played well for the assistant, because it became easier to open up to Mihai that many private Universities have higher taxes relative to the wages of the middle class. He confessed that he wants to create together a foundation. Mihai, who was always open towards ne, accepted Gabriel's proposal with the condition that Gabriel will be in charge with the formalities. He confessed also that uncle Flavius left in his will one million dollars for poor children and other charitable actions, Ana being the administrator of this money.

The news about the money left by uncle Flavius encouraged him and made him ready to start the work for foundation. After revolution the relations with the outside world became more democratic, in the sense that anyone could access money coming through banks.

Regarding the foundation he thought immediately that Mariana, his colleague, who was younger than him. He was in good relations with her. She sustained her doctoral thesis with Professor

Nita Dobrota, one of the most appreciated Professors from the Institute. While working at her thesis she consulted with Gabriel who provided her with foreign specialty journals. He was also selected in the doctoral commission, also because he was one of her referents. In the same commission was selected Professor N.N Constantinescu.

The thesis debate was very successful, and there after she has been promoted due to her achievements and for her connections.

She was very kind, calm; sometimes she was too serious for her age. She was very private with her personal life, which perhaps gave her some problems. Gabriel thought to have her work with him exactly because of her tempered qualities.

The foundation shouldn't be soothing that would attract a lot of attention, and its members should be selected carefully. The decided that the name would be "Our children", and its scope was only charitable; helping children of all ages from babies to students.

The statute of the foundation was drafted by Mariana and the president of the foundation was selected to be Ana Solomon from Israel who came with the money and the capital.

*

For Manea family the month of November looked as a photo album in warm colors. Doctor Teodor Manea will be 85 years old.

The twins Ana and Mihai were 50, and they couldn't meet in January. Now, when they'll celebrate their father's 85th birthday, they will celebrate their 50th and to it they added the Saints names Mihai and Gavril. All in all they decided to get together for a celebration of all.

The old place where Doctor Manea started his medical career was re-opened to a young family of doctors. Ana sent for them new modern medical equipment. It took a while for them to learn how to use it. The old Doctor Manea got himself involved in this task learning along with the young couple the new electronic technology. He didn't want to be too nosy, so he went to them once in a while even if they were neighbors.

Teodora wanted to organize this reunion for the whole family including the grandchildren; it passed some time since they got together as a whole family. Thinking at all the benefits that the revolution brought she was, in the same time, scared of it. She remembered the trauma that she had to endure during the war. These things she could not forget. Doctor Manea, also wanted badly to see his family too. 85 years of life for a man is a nice accomplishment and who knows when they'll meet again in the future.

Vasilica and Pricop died few years back. In their place came a young family from Ivanesti. The Doctor helped Tinca to get a job at a factory nearby for clothing, and her husband Grigore became a security man in the Central Square of Vaslui. They were living now in Vasilica's place and in their free time helped Teodora. The garden was well kept as it was always spring.

The hospital knew about the 85th birthday of Doctor Manea and his collaborators, colleagues, as well as Teodora's colleagues offered to help organize the festivities to celebrate this anniversary. Some of these volunteers showed up one day at Teodora's home asking how they can help. They put together a list of things to be done; bake, cook all sorts of goodies, and all traditional food. Teodora opposed, but she could not win... The volunteers wanted badly to help showing in this way their thanks to Doctor Manea who helped most of them in many occasions.

They decided that the festivities will take place on Saturday after noon. Ana, Horia, and their sons arrived in Bucharest several days before. Gabriel informed Ana about the foundation and that she is the President and the sponsor. They decided what the amount should be, and the account in which Ana will deposit the money for the "Our children" foundation. The judicial part of the foundation was Gabriel's job.

Friday morning the two cars loaded started to roll to Vaslui. Mihai and Gabriel were the drivers. In fife hours they reached their parents' house in Vaslui. Teodor Junior was already there.

The reunion was a very happy event when they saw each other; all the birds back to nest.

The father was overwhelmed with joy by the numerous gifts received: a Swiss watch, a robe of Chinese silk, a mobile phone and many other gifts from the grandchildren. There were gifts for mother and grandmother too: scarf, French fragrances, fur hat, and more.

The parents considered that it came the time to disclose to their sons and daughter, and open, perhaps for the last time the box with secrete memorabilia. They wanted to distribute the treasure left by Isidor and Berta about Ana and Mihai didn't know anything about its existence.

This surprise was scheduled to take place after the festive dinner; they mentioned to the twins that there are more deconspirate secrets than those provided at the time when uncle Flavius Solomon visited them. The twins agreed that some of the secrets shouldn't be divulged, because they maintained the unity and harmony in the Manea's family.

Saturday, day of celebration, selected carefully in the fall's calendar was blessed by nature. The garden smelled of ripen quince, pears and apples. The sun was sending its uniform rays and the wind from time to time was playing with the petals of the flowers. The chrysanthemums were the spoilers with their majestic slightly swaying, were enjoying the charm of the autumn copper.

Dressed in white as a bride, on the terrace was the big table, overfilled with the best cooked and baked dishes.

At the festive table was only the close family. Ana retained her glamorous image through the years. Perhaps, she discovered the youth elixir, and kept it secret until a presentation for Nobel Prize. She was wearing a blue dress and as during the student's years she looked as delicate sculpture. Horia, her husband, was to be 58 soon, however he didn't show it. His youth was streaming from inside and his life lines were irradiating only light.

Mihai was always a handsome gentleman. He belonged to that category of those who with age acquires extra charm. His salt and pepper hair was in in harmony with the blue metallic color of his eyes.

His wife Raluca, delicate as a swallow with piercing look, was guessing from the first view the hidden essence of the objects and surrounding beings. Her innate beauty was doubled by the refined way of dressing herself.

Gabriel, from early childhood was a daredevil often giving his parents scary dramas. When he grew up he became a vulture which never hunts flies. He liked to learn continuously splitting the hair in four until exhaustion. His brain never stopped thinking. Even as appearance he was different from the other brothers. He had a rich curly black hair, dark eyes, he looked like a personage from a poster with Tudor Vladimirescu unit.

He met Liliana in the first day when she moved in the Campus. Her parents died in a car accident when she was 15. She grew up paying attention to everything, and she was thinking twice before making a decision. When she met Gabriel she was very conservative. Gabriel with his athletic body, and academic career was spotted always by beautiful students. Liliana with a body as a vine, azure eyes could compete with any earthly beauty. She retained from Shakespeare that 'jealousy is a green-eyed monster which mocks us", and therefore she decided to stay away from this monster.

After Alesia got married, Liliana kind of got in the tumult, which actually was love, and decided to get guided by Gabriel who she trusted totally. They married late, when their relations became very strong and their professional careers were fulfilled.

The younger son, Teodor Junior (when he was little they called him Doru), was a dreamer, he seems absent from everything that happens around. In fact he was making notes in his mind, and no details were missing. He looked like Teodora. His face's lines were fine, sometimes feminine. His hands were delicate with long fingers, born namely for caressing the piano keys. It was a pity that in Vaslui wasn't a great music school for his talent; he would have been a great pianist. He dressed himself after the latest journal, the hair was nicely styled. He was handsome and walked carefully worried that something could go wrong with his hair dew.

He didn't have a girlfriend, although he passed well over forty. His brothers had some suspicions in relation to his orientation; same had his father, but Teodora considered that the boy is still a child.

The second generation (the grandchildren) reached also the maturity, they grew strong as the strong oak trees in the forest, with deep roots which could not be dislocated by the life tumult.

The grandchildren were exceeding the family expectations. Horace, the oldest, was doctor and was doing his specialization in a hospital in New York, living in the house of uncle Flavius. Ans was the one who insisted to come to the grandfather anniversary, because you never know when we'll get together again in his formation. Theodor, the younger brother of Horace, was also a doctor and he was leading the family private practice and worked also at the main hospital in Tel Aviv.

Raluca and Mihai's children, twins were two years younger. They chose different professions; Michael studied physics and specialization in the Netherlands in a secret research center. He didn't tell anyone what exactly he was working on. Physicists and engineers examined the theoretical conditions under which the universe was born.

In Switzerland, near Genera, under the mountains at about 10 Km deep, was constructed the largest particle accelerator in the world. The research is of a long duration and sometimes very risky. If the experiment succeeds or not it depends on the "God Particle" (Higgs boson).

Flavius, Michael's twin brother chose medicine, and was practicing at Elias Hospital.

The youngest Manea, granddaughter Maria, came into the picture like in a painting, ready to dance to the Spanish flamenco music. Gabriel was very proud that his daughter looks like him; she had black curly hair; grandmother fixed a white chrysanthemum flower behind her year. She was a freshmen student at the Academy for International Relations. She finished the Lyceum in German language and parallel she went to the music school. Professor Gabriel Manea was very proud of his beautiful and smart daughter Maria.

At first, the grandchildren felt discomfort and restrained, but quickly the discussions opened up. What a generation?

Horace saw Maria a couple of years back, when she was in High School. Then he didn't see her other than a normal school girl. Now, Maria was a revelation for him. He felt that only at Hollywood you can find such beauty. He listened to everything she was saying, word by word.

At the table the young generation nibbling on the delicious food, engaged in family conversations. At the end of this beautiful Saturday afternoon dinner, the grandparents offered to everyone surprising gifts which were part of the family secrets.

Mihai, the first born, received the "Star of David". No one asked why.

The gift passes from hand to hand arousing pleasant emotions. After being touched by everyone, the Star reached Mihai again. He squeezed it in his hands and experienced an unknown sentiment, which was electrifying him, and leaving a profound sentiment, for a moment, sister with the eternity, the mysterious sentiment of his communion with his parents and all his relatives. The Star – dematerialized – nestled like a heavenly light, in a special place, in his soul, receive a new moral responsibility.

Ana received a similar gift from uncle Flavius, at her wedding with Horia. She found this gesture very normal and she was happy that Mihai has received himself a similar gift.

Next, Teodora pulled from the leather bag another gift; this was for Ana. It was a very old collector's coin with the image of Maria Theresa, Empress of Austria in the second half of the eighteenths century. Looking at her face, once could see that she enjoyed the gift.

Horia received a coin with the effigy of Napoleon I. The coin was bright, although it was over a century old.

Gabriel and Teodor each received coins with the effigy of the Russian Czar Nicolae.

Raluca, Liliana and the grandchildren, each received one French cockerel, and Turkish coins.

None of the children, not even Ana and Mihai, who held the key of the secrets of Manea's family disclosed by uncle Flavius, didn't know about the hidden treasury for all these years. They, now, were thinking, what other secrets were there, about they didn't know? It seems that the parents will disclose them when time is right.

Next day Mihai, Ana, Horia and the parents left for Pungeşti to visit the tomb of their ancestors. Nobody asked why only they will go in this trip. The grandchildren preferred, any way to continue their conversations and the good time being together. Mihai took the Star of David in the inside jacket packet, next to his heart; it was his desire and supreme consideration, tradition, and faith for his forefathers. It seems that the forefathers were satisfied that the Star reached the right person.

At home, the grandchildren continued their party. Horace had eyes only for beautiful Maria, who was dressed as a young lady. Many around noticed the attraction, but didn't dear to comment. The girl was blushing every time he complemented her. Liliana watching her daughter remembered her first warm feelings for Gabriel. The father, who loved his daughter more than anything else remembered the time when Horia took Ana away to Israel. Then no one objected, even if Teodora and her husband, cried in silence, but respected the children decision. Their sister, Ana is happy and maybe that God wants a great love story to repeat itself.

Next day, those from Bucharest left first. Teodor Junior remained behind. He wanted to leave in the afternoon to Iassy. The trip would take him, approximately one hour and ½.

The separation was abundantly watered with tears. Who knows when they'll see each other and in what circumstances?

*

The two cars with the parents and children arrived safely in Bucharest. The young children organized their own accommodations. They all wanted to live with Uncle Gabriel and Ana and Horia at uncle Mihai, only Flavius who wasn't in vacation needed to report every morning to work, and therefore he withdrew to rest.

The rest of the group visited Bucharest's museums, guided by Maria and her good friend Silvia from music school, violin class. They both studied violin, then from fifth grade they both switched to piano. Maria didn't intend to make a musical career, even if she loved music. Silvia continued on the musical career path. In ninth grade they separated and went on different schools, but remained very good friends. After studies in Mathematics and Physics, Silvia returned to music enrolling at the Music Conservatory. She is with a girl with a lot of personality which can bring in the future advantages and disadvantages. Maria wanted to introduce her to her cousin, Theodor, the physician from Tel-Aviv but Silvia didn't want to commit.

In three days while they stayed in Bucharest, the girls enjoyed the company of the boys going to concerts and restaurants. After the boys left, Maria remained with some sort of nostalgia, thinking more often to Horace. Her parents did not know quite everything, but they had some suspicions. He was the first man to which she felt attracted. He on the other side talked to her about a lot of things, and promised her a lot of things, and sure enough Maria felled in love. . The e-mails and, phone conversations helped them to keep in touch often for hours.

A few months later Horace asked uncle Gabriel permission to spend the winter holidays in Bucharest. Obviously, his request was accepted. Ana, Horace's mother probably knew more, and wanted to come and wanted to come herself, because she was missing the Romanian Christmas traditions.

The holidays took place in family, at Vaslui. For Teodor Manea this was the last holiday spent in the family.

A few months later he left this world discreetly. Teodora found him in his armchair in the living room with a photo album on his lap. He, who saved so many hearts, suffered a cardiac arrest.

Shortly, after Teodora moved to Bucharest at Gabriel and Liliana. She wanted to be near Maria, who she loved so much. In the house at Vaslui remained two young couple from Ivanesti until one of nephews of Dragomir, professor, would receive the documents for the property. The only condition was that the relatives of Manea's family could come to Vaslui and live temporarily in their childhood house..

Maria and Horace were very much in love and they openly were together everywhere. Gabriel wanted to stop this love adventure because, actually they were relatives. Only Ana, was quiet and didn't worry a bit; Gabriel could not understand why?

The grandmother Teodora, due to the new situation created between the two lovers had to make another disclosure. The secret of Ana and Mihai was known only to them. If Gabriel would have known earlier this part of Manea's family secret, who knows what would have been his reaction; perhaps a total brake in their relation as a family.

Sometimes, in life, a lie the mother of bead, so badly heated, can gain the rank of queen, if it serves a noble cause, providing joy and happiness. Manea and Teodora decided to tell Gabriel an innocent lie for his protection, sustaining, in the same time, the strength of the family.

They told him that Ana is not their natural daughter, and she was found on the stairs of a church when she was only few months old. Being of the same age as Mihai they have been raised together as they were twins. Their advantage was that they both had blond hair. Therefore between Maria and Horace there is no blood relation. The parents asked Gabriel to keep this confidential, because, they claimed that Ana doesn't know.

Who knows when and how Manea's secret box will be opened again?

The winter holiday were going on. Horace got to know the Romanian traditions. Horace could come to Bucharest any time he wanted. Ana invited Maria and Liliana to Israel whenever they want.

When Maria was on her last year at the University, she and Horace got engaged. Her parents were laughing and crying in the same time. They hoped that Maria will remain in Bucharest professor at the Institute of Economic Sciences, as her father, but the events showed that things will take another course. Maria received her Master Degree from the University in New York with a scholarship from Israel, and her specialization at the World Bank.

Gabriel, sometime, in the past, dreamed that he'll work for the World Bank, but this dream disappeared as the time passed. But, Maria after specialization sure will fulfill her planes.

The professor was proud of the four students who received scholarships from the Foundation "Our children". He gave up teaching at the private University.

Codrin Apostol, his assistant, didn't keep the connection with the University. When the foundation started, Codrin made a substantial donation, making possible the scholarships for students.; he asked that his name to remain undisclosed.

*

The large waiting hall at the Otopeni airport was almost full. People of all age women and men were waiting to see their flights listed on the monitors. Children were frolicking in a small perimeter, when the announcer's voice was heard; they looked around to find out where the voices are coming from. They were looking at the people who were entering and exit through the three glass sliding doors. Security people were walking around.

On the side door entered two men, apparently of different age, it seemed to be father and son. On the shiny floor glided graciously a large luggage with silent wheels. On a label was visibly written O.M.S. The man who was guiding the luggage was around 60 years, tall slim, with a diplomat like allure; white shirt, red-burgundy tie, dark grey suite, and high vest completed his attire. His eye glasses with golden frames discretely protected his blue eyes, which were in a continuous movement. His son with few inches taller was the father mirror copy if you turn the time with thirty years back. The son had had blond hair and clear blue eyes. His attire was very casual –sport style which feet him well for travel. He had a jacket full of packets and zippers. His shirt unbuttoned at the neck. A large luggage was sliding almost alone on its wheels.

The airplane wasn't announced yet, the two men were looking around to find a place for conversation or perhaps for some other people who were travelling to the sunrise country. Their attire and good manners have been noticed immediately by other travelers.

Doctor Mihai Manea professor at the University of Medicine "Carol Davila', Correspondent member of Medical Science Academy and recently selected to represent Romania to OMS was travelling to Japan. His son Flavius, doctor at Elias Hospital, assistant Professor at the Medicine University was accompanying semi-official his father.

He took advantage of the travel arrangement of his father and took a couple of weeks off for special research for his doctoral theses, which had some tangent subject with the Japanese nutrition.

In the amalgamation of people was difficult to find such a place. Surprisingly the majority of passengers were young.

Next to a row of seats a gentleman rises, he was maybe of the same age as Mihai Manea. Looking at his posture and figure he seemed to be of German origin. He approached them and said

"Michael". Mihai was surprised, left the luggage in Flavius's care and hugged the gentleman the professor from Berlin Konrad Köller; they met few months before in Geneva at OMS session.

After greetings and hugging, the professor shakes Flavius hand, being certain that he is Mihai's son. All three went to the lounge to meet other two young doctors with he travelled.

Professor Köller was travelling to Japan for a research project, and the two young doctors were his assistance. The lady was Romanian from Bucharest, and because the professor didn't ever visited Bucharest accepted the invitation of his assistant and he was enchanted after he visited many historic museums and monuments. His assistant Zefi went to a German High School. After high school she went to the Medical University and her residency was done in Berlin, where she was very appreciated by the German colleagues and Professors. The young doctor's specialty was endocrinology, and she was working in the same time at her doctoral thesis. Zefi was not only smart and hardworking; she was beautiful, benefitted of physical qualities from her mother. Her slim figure and tender, as that of a dragonfly could be dressed from classic to extravagant. For this travel she opted for simple classic black pants, a white blouse which highlighted her youth. Her delicate young face didn't need any makeup. The natural lush of her cheeks was sufficient. Her black eyes as two sparkles were noticing everything that was surrounding her; this could be a professional deformation. Her colleague was of Indian origin. He seemed not to have any problems with the clothing; he resorted to the traditional Indian dressing. Next to Zefi was her brother who came to bring her to the airport.

The group became larger when a string quartet: two girls and two boys joined them. They were travelling also to Japan. Their attire was more of an artist, but not beyond a certain limit.

Zefi started the introductions; Sandra, her cousin, next to her, as a black bodyguard, inert was a black tall box made of fiberglass, large enough to protect the cello from external aggressors. Sandra tall and with a figure of a model was dressed in a sport suit, black, which was too sober for her youth but that was the fashion of the month. She had beautiful large brown eyes, a little of an almond shape, as she had some ancestors in orient. Her tall forehead was perfect integrated with the oval face with a very smooth skin as that of a child. Her black hair was combed in a small bun swirled like a snail caught only with a huge polished stick of wood, the Japanese style. Sandra was talking fast only in English holding close by her the cello box.

The other girl in the group was English, also tall and slim with a hair very blond. She was leaning on a smaller box for her violin. The American man from the group seemed to be a little older than the girls, but younger than thirty. The box of his violin was attracting everyone attention because of his personalized labels. The other young component of the quartet was Japanese, and probably he was going home.

Reserved in conversation was only Flavius Manea, who's English wasn't perfect, he was thinking first in Romanian.

The conversations stopped when the check in for Tokyo was announced. The American took Sandra's cello to help her out and gave her his violin. Followed then the routine checks and then the boarding. They maintained their group compact so they can chitchat during flight.

The night's cape was broken by the strong lighting of the airport. Those who came to accompany loved ones were still looking at the silver bird which was sliding on the runway preparing to take off as a comet.

The airplane raised flickering its lights and then disappeared when penetrated the puffy clouds splitting the sky blue waves, higher, higher, and higher!

www.ingramcontent.com/pod-product-compliance
Lightning Source LLC
Chambersburg PA
CBHW031350170626
46807CB00002B/904